The New Dawn

Book #4 in the
Comes the End series by
William Creed

ISBN 978-1-9393062-6-5

Printed in the United States of America
Published by 23 House Publishing
SAN 299-8084
www.23house.com

Author Contact:
wscreed@hotmail.com

Books of the Comes the End series:
Comes the End – Book One
The Gathering – Book Two
The Promise – Book Three
The New Dawn – Book Four

Other Books by the Author:
Faith: God's Gift

To My Wife

A word of thanks to my patient wife who doesn't nag me about mowing the lawn, cleaning the garage, or a million other things. She just patiently remains lovingly quiet allowing me to try and create my stories. Of course, when I'm done writing, she smiles and begins the required nagging.

A Word Of Thanks

I want to thank Alison Witt for her excellent editing of this manuscript.

Table of Contents

The Story Continues...

In *The Promise*, the third in the *Comes the End* series, Andy Moore, also known as The Prophet, is the leader of a group of Christians. Andy, with his wife Stephanie, was killed by Ramon, the Prefect of the area. They were delivered to the soldiers by Lorraine Eppinger and Sergeant Harkins. Lorraine is sent back to the mountain to tell the Christians that the soldiers are coming and none shall survive.

Meanwhile, Sergeant Harkins is beaten by men under the command of Sergeant Brunswick.

A report is received stating soldiers are nearing the summit of the mountain but have yet to run into any resistance, or sight of any inhabitants. Sgt. Brunswick is told to execute Harkins; however, Brunswick sees other opportunities and leads Harkins away from General.

Chapter 1: The Escape

Mary watched the crowd walking slowly towards the Great House. Despite knowing their deaths lay ahead, there were occasional tears of fear. Families reached out to one another, feeling by touching their loved ones, they could comfort the fears. Here and there many threw down their weapons as the long line walked slowly back to the center of camp. Knowing the Prophet and his wife were now dead was the final nail in their coffins. They knew soon the troops advancing below would soon be here.

Mary motioned to Roy Kegler. "Dad, could you drive me to the boat launch?"

"The boat launch? Why in the world would you want to go there now? This is no time for that! Honey, they're coming. We need to be together when they arrive."

"I know, and I will be there – but I need to go the water right now. I can't even tell you why, except I feel it's very important.

Kegler looked at his daughter for a moment before answering. "Okay, but we gotta go. Where's your mother?"

"She's coming right now."

As Betty Kegler approached she was joined by Reverend McDee. Immediately McDee, Roy, Betty, and Mary got in the electric cart. Seeing Tim, they hailed him to get in the small trailer the cart was towing.

Immediately, Roy got the former golf-cart headed for the lake. The whine of the electric motor wound down as they approached the road leading to the lake. After turning, it was only a short drive to reach the boat launch. There, Mary got out and gave Tim a kiss, and then reassured all she would meet them at the cabin within a few minutes. Tim started to get out as well, but Mary asked him to stay with the others.

3

After the cart started back, Mary walked to the peaceful water's edge – a stark contrast to the distant intermittent screams of fear and sorrow. It had been that way all day: flurries of excitement, and tears, followed by a period of ominous silence. The life they'd known was ending and their deaths, and the deaths of their children, lay ahead. The camp was surrounded by armed soldiers intent upon their destruction. It was only a matter of time until they decided to advance up the mountainside.

Reaching the water's sleepy edge, she carefully climbed in the nearest rowboat and sat down. She found that being pregnant and climbing into a rowboat didn't necessarily go together. Wrapping her arms around her raised knees, she laid her chin on them and looked out on the quiet waters. Despite the pending death, and the rumblings of the earth, she felt the quiet of the waters calming her soul.

"It is peaceful isn't it?"

The voice startled her. Looking up she saw the Prophet standing a few feet away.

"Oh, I'm so glad you're here! We were told the soldiers killed you. How did you get away?"

The Prophet smiled. "I didn't."

"I don't understand."

"I'm here to talk about what lies ahead," Andy said as he retrieved a flat stone from the beach. Carefully he threw it at the water and watched as it skipped. "I've gotten better at that," he smiled. Then, looking at Mary, he sighed. "God's hand is on you, Mary. You were chosen long before you were born, chosen for this very day and hour. Do you know that?"

"I feel God's hand upon me. I felt that way since I can remember, long before you and Stephanie came here. My father and mother told me that. But, something is bothering me. My baby has not yet drawn a breath, and soon she will die when I do. My question is this: What will happen to her soul? Will she be with us in heaven?"

4

"Every soul that was created by God and placed in a human body will live again to face God. Remember that Mary; it's important that you remember."

"Why?"

"I haven't come to talk to you about this. Everything in its time and this is not the time. Now I want to tell you that God has been preparing you all your life for the days that lie ahead. I've come to tell you about your next task. You are to lead some out of here, while others will see the Lord today."

For a moment, Mary was silent. "But I've been preparing myself to meet Jesus today, and I think I've come to the point of being ready, even looking forward to it a little." She paused. "Does that sound crazy?"

"No, not at all, though to some, it might seem that way. For us who know there is a wonderful life waiting beyond, we know not to fear death, but look upon it as a doorway into a spectacular tomorrow for our souls. You see, Mary, after the great snatching of souls, there are so many who will be left behind, and regret their choices. They've come to want to give their hearts and souls to Christ, but feel left out. You and others are their hope."

"I don't understand."

"You are not supposed to understand, you are supposed to believe – yours is to have faith that God will lead you, and He will."

Mary nodded.

Andy threw another stone and it skipped once and sank. After letting Mary absorb what he said, he continued.

"Soon you must leave here."

"How can that be? We are surrounded by soldiers. There are even reports some of their patrols have made it near the camp in preparation for a final attack."

The Prophet smiled. "All the reports are true. But don't let facts get in the way of your faith. The time for fear has passed; the time for your tomorrow is here. You are to lead some to

5

safety, but listen: You are not to ask anyone to follow. Those who are to leave with you will come to you. I tell you this – God's hand is upon you. He will guide you. However, while His hand leads, you must be willing to follow in faith. Do not allow the fears of today to destroy yesterday's faith, for they are the cornerstones of tomorrow's joys. For if your faith is lost, so shall be those in your charge." With that, the image of the Prophet faded.

"Wait!" said Mary, jumping up. The motion made the boat tilt, almost dumping her into the water. Carefully stepping out onto the beach, she sank to her knees praying for strength and wisdom. Then rising, Mary broke into a run as she made her to her cabin.

As she approached she saw that Tim was waiting for her along with Reverend McDee. Quickly she and Tim embraced. "It's time for me to leave," said Mary.

"Leave?" asked Tim, with some astonishment. "How can we leave? There are soldiers everywhere! I think we need to get some guns. I saw a bunch of people headed for the chapel, and we need to join them."

"I repeat, it's time for me to leave," replied Mary. "I'm not asking anyone to go with me."

"To where?"

"Wherever God leads us," replied Mary, then turned to Tim with a questioning look.

Tim smiled, "You and I are one, Sweetie. Where God leads you, I will go."

"If you think your mama is gonna watch you go," smiled Betty, "you got another think comin' – right, Daddy?"

"You got that right," smiled Roy.

"Food. We're gonna need food," said Mary.

"The garden," volunteered Tim. "I'm sure we'll find something there we can pack to take with us – at least enough for a few days."

Leaving the house, they found their electric cart was gone, but saw it when reaching the Great House where the four-seater, with its small trailer, sat unattended. The Great House still was being slowly consumed by flames, though they were now less energetic and more smoke than flame could be seen. Tim, Mary, McDee, and Betty got in with Roy getting into the trailer. Steering the cart out onto Great Circle Drive, Tim headed for the garden. They passed a line of people walking towards the Great House singing hymns. As they watched, two of them threw their rifles on the ground.

Tim stopped the cart. "What are you doing – you're gonna need them!" said Tim, pointing to the firearms.

"No," a passing woman smiled, "we won't need them."

"Look," said Roy pointing to a number of other guns on the ground.

"Pick them up and get any ammo belts too!" shouted Tim as he jumped out of the cart. "We'll need them for sure."

The group scooped up a dozen firearms as the stream of people, continuing to sing, passed on their way to the Great House.

Suddenly, Rachelle Myers came running towards them with the twins trying hard to keep up. "Tim, Tim!" she yelled as she drew near with tears running down her cheeks. "Tim," she gasped trying to swallow her tears and gulp oxygen. "I want you to take my girls – hide them!"

"What? Come with us," said Tim

"I cannot. I can't explain, but please, I beg you, hide my babies – please."

Tim glanced at his wife and her mother and it was clear want they wanted him to do. Holding out his hand he said, "Here – come here, girls."

Katie hesitated. "Where are you going, Mama?"

Rachelle's sobs made speech hard. "I'm going to be with Daddy, honey. Don't worry, I'll be watching." She then kissed Katie and Alison, and before they could respond, turned and ran

7

off toward the Great House which still had flames licking some standing boards.

For a moment little Katie hesitated. Thinking she might be about to run after her mother, Tim jumped out of the cart and scooped up Katie, hugging her. "Don't cry, sweetheart, everything will be alright in the end."

"I don't get it, why won't she come?" said Roy, then, turning to Mary, "Do you?"

Before Mary could answer, Tim interrupted. "I do – I heard the story – I'll tell you later."

"We need to get going!" said Ray.

The small group got back into their cart and drove toward the garden. Twice the ground beneath them moved as they were driving, causing the cart to swerve dangerously. Arriving at the stairway to the garden, they began the short, but steep, climb.

"Girls!" admonished Betty Kegler to the eight-year-old twins. "You put those guns down this instant! Roy, aren't you watching them? Do you want them dead before we start?"

Roy bent down, smiling as he took the two pistols from the twins.

"Oh, no!" came Tim's shout from above.

Quickly the rest joined him and saw the reason for his dismay. The once-beautiful garden was now a sorry excuse for its once-healthy and abundant self. The leaves were brown and withered – those that weren't already lying on the ground.

"What happened?" asked Betty

"It's the time," came a voice from behind them.

Turning, they saw a withered old man, looking much like the plants surrounding them. Though he was standing, he was bent over so far it was doubtful he could see who he was addressing.

"There's a time for life and a time for death," he added flatly.

"I know who you are – the Prophet told me about you!" blurted Mary. "You're the one he called the Hermit."

8

"Some call me that, yes they do," he said with wrinkles crinkling into a possible smile. "So, you folks need some traveling food – well, if you go back of them bushes over there you'll find a few healthy corn stalks. There're a couple of bean plants and tomatoes too. I think they'll get you by for a little."

Suddenly the ground beneath them moved. The twins and Betty let out a short cry.

"What is it?" squeaked little Alison.

"It feels like an earthquake," responded Tim with some concern.

"Yep, sure enough does," added the Hermit. "I think you best get your food and leave."

"But where?" asked Betty, of no one in particular.

Mary stood up with a few stalks of corn in her hand. "Look, all we have to do is put one foot in front of the other, and the only option open is forward and down the other side of the mountain."

"That's it?" asked Roy in a fatherly tone. "Look, Mary, I know the Lord speaks to you, but that's all He's said?"

"Well, if you don't mind my making suggestions, I do think I know a way for those footsteps," replied the Hermit.

The group turned towards him with their vegetables.

"Down the back side of this mountain – down where the caves are – I know of a way. And at the bottom there aren't many soldiers."

"Wonderful!" said Mary. "Will you show us?"

"I'd be happy to do that, but we better get going," he said as the ground trembled again.

Using shirts and sweaters, they bundled their veggies and followed the Hermit. For his obvious age, he was quite agile leading them down the mountain. Every fifty feet or so, he would pause to see if the others were keeping pace. When they came to caves they paused allowing everyone to catch their breath.

At the third cave, the Hermit sat longer than usual.

9

"Some reason we aren't going?" asked Tim.

Hermit nodded. "Our transportation hasn't arrived."

"Our transportation? You know of some transportation?"

The Hermit nodded. "They don't know it yet, but they'll learn."

"I don't mean to question," Tim began, "but I'm surprised the soldiers haven't seen us up to now. It seems we've been in plain sight."

The Hermit nodded. "Yes, sometimes our eyes just don't see what we think they should." Again his wrinkles crinkled.

A few minutes later the twins crawled over to the Hermit and sat facing him.

"My sister and I have been wondering, is your name Hermit or Kermit?"

"Well, I've been called many names. Would you like to call me Kermit?"

Alison nodded. "I know someone else named Kermit and he is very good."

"In that case I would be honored to be Kermit."

"I remember hearing about you in camp," she smiled.

"Um-hmm," responded the Hermit.

"Some people say you are an angel. Are you an angel, Kermit?"

"Well now, I hear angels are just the prettiest things – have you heard that?"

"Yes, they are pretty."

"Well, in that case, I would say you're closer to being an angel than I."

"But you know everything."

"Oh, now don't go saying that, I only know what I'm told and I'm only told what I need to know."

Mary approached. "Sir, it's getting dark. Should we be leaving?"

"Mary," said Alison with a smile, "he told me I could call him Kermit."

10

"What?" asked Mary. "Who's Kermit?"

"Yep, about time to get moving," said the Hermit looking out at the graying sky and dark shadows now covering this side the mountain. Nodding, he repeated, "Yep, time to get moving. Think so."

As he got up, Alison and Katie could be heard arguing in whispers. "I told you, he's Kermit," hissed Alison.

"Don't be stupid, he's too ugly to be Kermit – everyone knows that," Katie hissed back.

Slowly, using his cane, the Hermit headed for the fading daylight. Outside the cave he looked back, assuring himself that his charges were following.

"Now friends, this is a difficult part of our journey. You are going to see a lot of soldiers, but fear not; however, you must be quiet." With these last words, he looked at the twin girls who nodded in return.

Suddenly, the ground moved again. This time the movement was sudden and very jerky. A few boulders from above could be heard rolling down the mountainside. The twins squealed as did Betty.

The Hermit turned towards them raising his finger to his lips. Slowly he led the group towards the level ground below Occasionally hopping from stone to stone as though forgetting his age, then looking back to see if his charges were able to follow. They all could see soldiers a few hundred yards away, but they passed them unnoticed. Soon, but not as soon as wished, they were at the bottom. Here, raising his cane the Hermit signaled all to get down. He then went onto the gravel road. Tim looked back and up to the top of the mountain and Camp Noah. There were wisps of smoke beginning to lay upon the peak with some wisps drifting downward.

The sound of an approaching vehicle signaled everyone to hug the ground. The sound revealed an army-brown military truck. Suddenly a tire exploded, and the truck veered to the left almost hitting a tree.

11

For a moment, all was quiet, and then the Hermit began walking towards the vehicle. Mary could see two soldiers in the truck, and was tempted to yell out to the Hermit, but remained quiet. One of the soldiers got out and began inspecting the deflated tire unaware of the approaching Hermit.

Chapter 2: The Pursuit

It wasn't until the Hermit was almost to the truck before either of the soldiers noticed him. Looking at the driver, he said, "I see you got a problem here."

Harkins was in no mood for small talk with an old wrinkled man. Suddenly his memory was jogged as he recognized the Hermit. "Well, I'll be. I know you! Yes, sir. You're from the camp up there aren't you?" he said with a smile. "I remember seeing you once and then hearing about you from others."

"Yes, and I got some passengers for you. They need to get somewhere, and here you are."

"Passengers? No, no sir, I can't have any passengers. They will be hunting for us and surely will find us here because with this tire we're not going anywhere."

"Yep. That's true," said the Hermit, then turning his attention towards Sergeant Brunswick, "I see you have brought someone."

"This is Sergeant Brunswick," smiled Harkins. "He helped me escape."

The Hermit looked at Brunswick for a moment without comment, then turned back towards the road and waved his arm, signaling the others to join them.

Seeing the Hermit wave, Mary stood up, and then winced.

"What's wrong Honey?" asked Tim

"Oh nothing, I just think the baby wants me to stop running around," she smiled.

Reaching the truck, Tim looked at the tire. "Well, I don't think we are going anywhere."

Harkins nodded. "I looked for a spare, but this truck doesn't have one. I can't believe it – it's not like this man's army to send out a truck without a spare."

"Oh, don't you never mind about that," replied the Hermit. "I think this tire will do just fine."

13

"Oh my God!" exclaimed Harkins as he saw the flat tire was now fully inflated. "How did that happen?"

"Let's not dwell on unimportant things," said the Hermit. "It's time you all get in this truck and get going. It won't be long before some unwanted visitors may be coming down this road."

Sergeant Harkins climbed in behind the wheel. Brunswick started to get in the passenger side, but was interrupted by the Hermit. "Sergeant, if you don't mind. I think it would be best if Tim and Mary sat up front."

Brunswick hesitated a moment. "Oh, of course, that would be fine," he said as he dismounted, and held the door open for Mary, followed by Tim.

Harkins started the truck as Mary settled carefully into the passenger seat.

"Sir," said Mary leaning towards the passenger window, "Aren't you coming?"

The Hermit's face crinkled a bit. "No. Now you get as far away from this mountain as you can. Where you need to go will be shown you. Remember you are on a journey of faith."

"Yes," nodded Mary.

"Two more things you must keep in mind. Not everyone who calls you a friend is a friend, and second, your gifts will return. Use them."

"My gifts? What are you talking about?"

The Hermit did not answer but stepped back as Harkins applied the gas and the truck pulled out on the highway.

As they pulled away Mary looked back to wave goodbye but the Hermit was gone.

Driving, they discovered the truck had unforgiving springs and Tim asked Sergeant Harkins to slow down for Mary's sake, though she was not complaining

"Where are we headed?" asked Tim.

Harkins thought a moment, "You know I'm not really sure – just away from this mountain right now."

"If I may make a suggestion," began Mary. "I recall the Prophet telling of an experience he had near here off US 85. He said there was a river which ran alongside the highway where we could travel out of the view of searching eyes."

"Yes, I recall him talking about it, too. But didn't he say that the river was subject to flooding when it rained? As I remember, he and Stephanie were almost killed when it flooded on them. And," he added, looking at the sky, "it looks like it's getting pretty dark, and I don't mean just the ash. Those look like storm clouds."

"It will be a good place for us to travel. We will be alright." said Mary, showing some authority in her voice, "I feel we will be alright," she repeated.

Sergeant Harkins turned onto Highway 280 and, ten minutes later, onto Highway 85. Within a few miles, Tim spotted the beginning of the guard railing and the river below. Searching for the right place, Harkins slowly guided the truck over the bank and downward. He was careful to keep the truck at right angles for it was top-heavy, and suspected if he were to steer parallel the truck would surely roll over. There were two levels to the river's bank, which he negotiated, finally reaching the river bed where the ground leveled out.

"Let's all get out and stretch our legs for a moment," suggested Harkins. "We are a little distance from the mountain."

"Yes, but I think all the ash in the air will bring darkness sooner than usual," said Betty Kegler.

Suddenly, as though a huge bomb had exploded, there was a flash of light as bright as a noonday sun.

Betty and the young girls let out screams as both Black Mountain and Cloud Mountain exploded as one. For a moment, the small group was transfixed by the horrific site.

"Into the truck!" shouted Mary finally.

From one of the mountains, the heights of which were now shrouded in thick black smoke, came a loud high pitched,

15

stream as super-heated gas shot skyward reaching thousands of feet within moments. The sound of the escaping steam grew in intensity. The piercing wail was so loud Betty, Mary, and the girls covered their ears. The white steam shot straight up until encountering currents of the upper atmosphere, which flattened it into an anvil cloud that began spreading out covering the entire area.

"We haven't much time!" yelled Harkins.

The tops of both mountains disappeared inside black billows, while red-hot lava shot upward disappearing into the smoke and flame. The lava fell and a stream of its redness began running down the sides.

As one, they all scrambled to the truck which Harkins had pulling away before Tim could close the passenger door. Within the next few minutes, smaller rocks from the distant explosion began raining down upon them. Harkins steered the truck toward the edge of the gully which was slightly concave, allowing some shelter from the rock raining down upon the river.

"Keep driving, Scott!" yelled Mary to Harkins.

Chapter 3: Kill All

Brigadier General Tony Valice instructed his driver to slow down as he drove the streets of downtown Laughton, Tennessee. The town had grown over the years, from a sleepy village of two thousand, to triple its size, all due to its location near Smith AFB. As they traveled the streets he found no signs of panic, all seemed to be their normal sleepy selves. It was a testimony to Valice's leadership in reassuring the town all was safe, despite the worldwide flurry of volcanic eruptions including one some two hundred miles to the east at Cloud Mountain. When the volcano exploded it brought with it an eruption of nearby Black Mountain as well. Fortunately for the town, the wind blew most of the toxic black ash and debris to the east.

Valice closed his eyes as he tried getting his mind around the world-wide devastation brought on by the simultaneous eruptions of so many active and dormant volcanoes. Scientists were going wild with theories, from new subterranean lava flows activated by a shift in the Earth's core, to changes in the relationship of the earth and moon. Their predictions for the future ranged from the volcanoes simmering down, to the planet blowing apart.

Add to that the cries of religious fanatics claiming it was God's judgment upon earth as foretold in the book of Revelation. Dealing with the facts was bad enough without a bunch of religious jerks stirring the pot. Of course, the networks were lapping it up with specials predicting when and where future disasters might occur – and selling millions in advertising while doing it.

"Okay, Sergeant, take me to the Fort," Valice said, satisfied the town was not in panic mode, or at least, not yet.

Fort Smith was a fairly new installation built for the demands of modern times. It consisted of roads running in

17

connecting circles, each circle housing different units with the center circle devoted to Administration. As he passed through the outer circles he again saw no signs of panic, although there had been reports of tensions within the camp growing.

Finally, arriving at the inner Command circle, the road circled around a fairly large inner area which allowed choppers to land.

As his car came to a stop in front of the building of his Central Command, Valice didn't wait for the driver to open the door, but hopped out and quickly climbed the four cement steps to the front doors. His offices were the first doors on the left entering the building. Arriving, he motioned Sergeant Sterling to follow him.

Inside his office, Valice rubbed his hands together. It was getting chilly. So many volcanoes becoming active and spewing dark, dangerous ash into the air caused the temperatures to fall. And, it was said, worse was to come. Though there was not much in the atmosphere above them, it was coming from the west and would affect them sooner than later.

"Sterling," he snapped, "have you heard from Captain Bellmore?"

"Yes, sir. Said they can't get within a couple miles of the mountain. The heat is too great. He did say they saw no sign of life whatsoever."

"I can't believe it. Decker is gone and not only that, the Prefect – what's his name?"

"Ramon, sir."

"Yeah, Ramon – everyone just swallowed up!"

"It's been happening all over the world sir."

Valice nodded while deep in thought. "The men, what do you get from the grapevine on the troops?"

"They're scared."

Valice nodded. "Yes, of course."

"Some say it's the end of the world."

"Nonsense," snorted Valice.

"And some," Sterling paused for a moment, anticipating the General's reaction. "Some say it's just like the Bible says."

"Don't go spewing that Bible Scum garbage! The last thing we need is a bunch of religious fanatics running around stirring up trouble!" He emphasized the last by hitting his desk with his fist.

"Well, sir, and I only say it in order to inform you of the situation, some are using the word 'Rapture'."

"Rapture? What's that?"

"It's part of the fanatic's religion. They think all Christians will be snatched from the earth just before earth blows up."

"Oh, come on, how many would believe that? I don't want any soldier spewing that garbage. If anyone does, he is to be removed from his unit permanently."

"Yes, sir."

"What we need to do is round up some of those Christian workers and bring them here. Parade them in front of the men and let them see who's boss. Let them see no snatching is going on around here."

"Well sir, now that's some bad news: They seem to have escaped."

"What are you talking about?"

"It's just like I said, they're gone – run off."

"There aren't any in the camp?"

"No, sir."

"I informed Captain Bellmore, and he's sent out some patrols to see if they can pick up any signs of where they may have gone. I think the worst scenario would be if they all went in different directions. Having to send out so many troops to hunt them down would be difficult."

Valice nodded. "Yes, but we'll do whatever we have to do. I don't want the word to get around that this escape was successful. Can you imagine what those Space Jockeys would say?"

Suddenly the intercom buzzed.

Valice slammed the button, clearly annoyed, and even more annoyed because his outburst of profanity would have to wait.

"What is it?" he snarled.

The voice on the other end was clearly shaken.

"Sir, you have some Ancestral Brother Visitors."

"The Brothers?" he asked, his voice subduing as he spoke.

"Yes, sir, they're in black robes and all."

"Show them in immediately," responded Valice, while straightening his fatigues. Just what he needed, some of those jerks showing up.

The door opened and two, very tall, black-robed figures entered, followed by a third in a red robe with black trim.

"Welcome," smiled Valice as he stepped forward, instinctually raising his hand, but awkwardly lowered it when there was no response.

The red-robed individual stepped from behind to face Major General Valice, and then pushed back his hood. "Hello General Valice," he growled while looking around. My name is Durk; I am the temporary Prefect for this area. The past Prefect, Ramon, was tragically killed in one of the eruptions we've all heard about."

"Yes, I was sorry to learn of this," responded Valice.

"I wanted to come by and introduce myself, to assure you, and those who serve you, that there is no cause for alarm, as it should be. When Abdon, who serves our supreme leader, Abaddon, came here he warned everyone upon the Earth that natural destruction of the planet was at hand."

"Yes, sir, I remember."

"This is just the first of many tragedies which shall befall the Earth. The time is even more critical than ever that we bring people together, for we must prepare to leave this planet."

Prefect Durk took a deep breath before continuing. "You know, we all know, what is delaying our departure."

Valice nodded, becoming more comfortable with the Prefect. "Yes, those God People, of course – especially the Christians."

"There are rumors running around that many of Christians have been rescued, like their comic book Bible says – which is ridiculous, of course. However, there seems to have been a mass conspiracy to perform an escape to the hills, or perhaps to prearranged hiding places within the countryside, or even the cities."

"Sergeant Sterling and I were just talking about some Christians who had escaped from my command. You say that others have escaped from different districts?"

Durk nodded. "So it appears; however, it is critical this ridiculous rumor stating their so-called God has rescued them cannot be allowed to stand. It is absolutely critical to recapture them, and to publicly execute them. Do I make myself clear?"

"Yes, sir, absolutely."

Valice turned and went behind his desk, but remained standing. "I hadn't considered a coordinated planned escape," he repeated slowly. "But now, when you say it, that seems a good explanation."

"There's another rumor going around, and I have yet to confirm this, that the escapees have put the Marks on their hands to deceive us. They seem to have planned on hiding among your people."

Sterling gasped. "But I thought their religion would prohibit that."

Durk whipped around to Sterling, obviously annoyed. "When you humans are confronted with death, your silly religion is out the window! Clearly, they fear death more than their invisible god. Now, what would be your plan to recapture them?"

"Certainly, we have to send our patrols to track them down; however, considering how many have escaped, I think a full mobilization is in order. I think I will contact General

21

Tucker of District Six for additional help. But if they now are bear the Mark, how are we to know which are which?"

"You figure that out – you're a General, right? You figure it out!" Something that could have been a grin crossed Durk's face. Quickly it disappeared before speaking again. "Shortly Abdon will speak to the world over your television sets. Make sure you are listening."

"But we can't – the cable is out."

"Your television will receive this message." Again his face contorted into a possible grin. "We have our ways. Let me say just one more thing. I am the Temporary Prefect of this area as well as temporary Commander of District Five. We are looking to find someone to become the permanent Prefect. Your rank of Brigadier General, along with your work thus far makes you a good prospect. Also, we are bringing all the District Commanders of my command to the Pyramid in your Mediterranean. Area Five has been particularly difficult, but with the proper leadership, I believe we can solve the problem, right General?"

For a second Valice was speechless at the implications of a possible promotion. "Yes...yes, of course. I will be more than happy to come, and you can count on me to do all that's necessary to bring the Christian trash to justice!"

Without waiting for Valice to finish, Durk turned, putting up his hood and leading the two other Visitors out of the office.

Both Valice and Sterling were silent for a moment after the door closed. Finally, the General swore softly, saying "Did you hear all of that, Sterling?"

"Yes, sir."

"I could be the new Prefect. Do you know what that would mean? Why there are only three Prefects for the USA, no more than three dozen for the entire planet! Get hold of Captain Bellmore immediately!"

* * * * *

22

The shallow river bed proved to be solid, allowing Harkins to drive as fast as sixty miles per hour in some spots. Finally, after driving several miles he slowed and brought the truck to a stop.

"I think we will be safe here," said Harkins, with Tim and Mary mumbling their agreement.

Their passengers filed out of the truck into the fading light, joining together in watching the red ribbons of lava inching down the sides of the mountains. The black cloud, which had been advancing towards them, was losing its energy and settling a few miles behind them. The evening quickly became night as the setting sun was completely blocked by the volcanic ash in the air.

"Well, what now?" asked Harkins.

From behind, they heard the voice of Sergeant Brunswick. "What about the other camps – maybe we can find some help there – at least be able to spend the night in one."

Mary stepped forward. "I don't think we've formally met yet. My name is Mary, and this is my husband, Tim."

Brunswick wiped his hand on his uniform before shaking their hands. "Sergeant Doyle Brunswick is the name, I knew Sgt. Harkins back there in the camp."

"Yes," said Harkins. "If it wasn't for Doyle I would be back on that mountain and called 'toast'."

"Well, to answer your question Sergeant Doyle, there are actually four camps: Adam, James, Jeremiah, and Noah. Noah is the one that was on top of that mountain."

"Are the others near here?" asked Doyle.

"Yes," said Mary. "One is Camp Adam. We should be able to reach it in with a couple of hours, but I don't think it will be wise. If they brought the army to Camp Noah, perhaps the others were visited also."

"Do you know how to get there?" asked Brunswick. "I heard the army knew about the camps, but not the location."

"Yes, perhaps we'll check them out later."

"Well, if you can get us near there, I think Harkins and I can scope it out while the rest of you wait a distance away."

Mary nodded slowly. "It's worth a chance, worth checking out – but I don't feel now is the time."

With that, the others began making their way back to the truck. Mary put her hand on Tim, restraining him.

"What is it?" asked Tim.

"That man – Brunswick."

"Yes?"

"I don't feel right about him."

"Really? Why?"

"Remember I told you when I was blind I could sense evil?"

Tim nodded.

"Well, when I gained my sight, I lost that ability – but I think I may have just felt it again."

"With Brunswick?"

Mary nodded.

Chapter 4: Bounty Hunters

Donald Denson was his given name; however, friends and family knew him as Donny Boy, despite his being seventy-six years old. When young he was chided about his name, but as the wrinkles grew the comparisons faded.

Before the Ancestral Brothers, most mornings saw Donny out in the field tending to his farm off Highway NC62. Over the years, he mostly farmed tobacco, but when so many kicked the habit, he was forced to change with the market. His hundred acres became two crops that grew well in the North Carolina soil – sweet potatoes and cucumbers. Ten years ago, he added some cattle and increased his chickens to seventy-five, give or take, but all that happened before the Ancestral Brothers came.

Now, over the last few years, the markets were messed up. Donny Boy couldn't sell his cash crops because there wasn't transportation to pick them up, and no transportation because there weren't market wholesalers, and no wholesalers because no retail markets, and no retail because customers had no money. Now, every morning he would grab his rifle for protection and walk to the field where he and Margie grew enough for their own consumption. The cattle were long gone, confiscated by the army, as were most of the chickens, although he did have four chickens and some chicks left, which the soldiers missed or couldn't capture.

Donny looked at the smoking volcanoes in the distance and the gathering blackness from the eruptions. At first he thought it was headed for them, but the prevailing winds stopped the soot and now the blackness seemed to be drifting to South. Nevertheless, he had decided to take precautions this morning in case the ash changed directions. Using feed, he lured the chickens and their new chicks into a wire cage. Then, picking up the cage, he headed back to the house.

On the porch, Donny set the cage down and checked the house windows making sure they were properly boarded, strong enough to withstand weather but, more importantly, unwanted hands. Though the windows were boarded, they were not tight. In fact, Donny left openings where he could peer out, including some flaps which allowed a defense of the house.

Releasing these flaps allowed his and Margie's rifles to poke out and fire if necessary.

If the ash made it to the house, Donny had decided to nail garbage bags up to block the windows. He didn't know much about volcanoes and the stuff that came out of them, but he knew it wasn't good. Whether garbage bags would do anything he wasn't sure, but so far it was all he'd come up with. The most vulnerable part of the house was the side door. Here, both the wood outside and inner screen door opened freely; however, inside double plywood sheets were cut and drilled to fit onto pre-fitted bolts which could hold securely under all but the most violent assaults. These precautions were necessary to defend against roaming gangs that were out to pillage homes. He heard they were in the area, though none had come yet. Additionally, he boarded the house so it would look deserted, or so he hoped.

Opening the door, he brought the chickens down to the basement where the floor was still earthen. He'd prepared a spot for the chickens should the volcanic ash reach them and surrounded it with a short wire fence. The eggs, and possibly the chickens, would be good food sources if worse days should come. Still, it was clear their chances of survival were slim and depended on surviving the black soot, roaming gangs, and army raids – all likely to return in the future.

Lora, his eight-year-old granddaughter, watched as the chickens began to investigate their new digs. Donny was sure Lora's parents were gone; either they were dead or on a never-ending chase of a dream. They were chasing those utopia-promising-jerks from space. Oh, they said they would return when they got their tickets to paradise, but neither Donny nor his wife, Mary heard from them again. They were not unlike many people who gave up their lives to chase after the promises. The usual result was they found it was a dead-end chase and resulted in cold and starving endless days. At that point, they either committed suicide or joined so many others who decided that taking what they needed or wanted was the way to go. They became Goonies. In fact, there were those on the television touting this very thing, claiming those who had been successful in life were evil and they had made it off the labor, misfortune, and exploitation of others. There were a significant number of people who subscribed to this view and used it to justify stealing the things they wanted.

While most were located in the city where the picking was good, others made it out to the country where the competition for the spoils was less.

Donny looked down at his granddaughter. He was committed to her survival – it was why he got the Mark.

"I'll feed them, Grandpa," Lora said, grabbing some feed and throwing it on the dirt. "It's getting awful dark out there, Grandpa, is it gonna rain?"

Donny grunted his usual initial response before speaking. "Oh, hope not."

* * * * *

It was late afternoon by the time Mary and the others drove out of the riverbed onto deserted Highway 62 going east. Because of a few wisps from the eruption drifting this far, the sun's rays were muted. The truck's cab was silent as Harkins drove. Everyone, including the children in the back, was absorbed in his or her own thoughts, fears, or an exhausted sleep. Once the initial escape from the camp succeeded, and the tension of it subsided, thoughts went to the future. Where they were going and what they would do when they got there, was unknown.

27

How would they keep hidden from the Goonies and Army? It was the Goonies though, that concerned Mary the most. They had no rules, and their tactics were brutal: however, none could argue against the success they had in rooting out Bible Thumpers and eliminating them. The army paid the bonus without any questions asked, as long as the severed hands did not have the Mark. It was not only finding someplace to hide from the Goonies and military that worried her – there was another force they had to take into consideration. The evil that lay upon the earth was a continual presence. It was important they keep their spiritual armor around them.

Finally, Mary broke the silence. "We are going to need a place to stay tonight. Keep your eyes open for a deserted structure."

A few moments later, Tim pointed to their left at a house showing signs of once being on fire, but that still looked intact. Mary was silent for a few moments as she studied the burned structure.

"I don't think so, honey. It doesn't feel right."

No one argued the judgments of Mary, for they all knew God's hand was upon her. She was the spiritual guide of the group and her connection with God's spirit was unchallenged.

As they drove further they passed several farms, but at each one Mary shook her head repeating, "It didn't feel right."

Twenty minutes later they spotted a farmhouse which was almost completely boarded up. There didn't appear to be any damage to it, or to the barn behind it.

"Slow down, Scott," Mary said to Harkins, and then motioned to stop the truck. Opening the door, she got out and walked a couple of steps ahead of the truck while looking around slowly. Finally, she walked back. "I think this might be the place – it feels right."

Harkins exchanged glances with Tim. It was still hard for him to give up the logical analyses that had governed his life in the military to this point, and instead surrender to Mary's 'feel right' judgments. However, Tim seemed comfortable, so he nodded for Harkins to go ahead. Harkins slowly pulled into the long driveway leading to the house about a hundred yards away. Slowly he inched down the gravel drive, concerned the house wasn't as deserted as it appeared. It might even be a citizen fortress and even now they could be coming into someone's rifle sight.

* * * * *

"Donny Boy!" shouted Margie down the stairs. "Somebody's coming!"

As quickly as his seventy-six-year muscles would allow, Donny made his way up the stairs, grabbing his rifle as he arrived in the kitchen. Running to the living room he peered out between boards and watched as the army truck pulled into their drive.

"The army – they're back," said Margie with disgust in her voice.

The truck stopped halfway to the house.

"Tell ya, honey, I don't know which is worse – the army or the Goonies."

"Let's hope it's not Goonies."

"Lora!" shouted Donny to his granddaughter. "Get downstairs. Remember how we practiced, and don't make a sound!"

Following his granddaughter to the kitchen, he watched as she disappeared down the stairs. Carefully, Donny replaced a rug over the kitchen floorboards, and the stairway that they covered, and then put the kitchen table on top. Quickly he went to the outside kitchen door and installed the bolted plywood sheets.

"What are they doing now?" he asked as he tightened the bolts.

"Nothing, just sitting there."

After arranging the table, Donny ran to join her.

As they watched, the truck began to move slowly forward. Then, again it stopped, halfway down the drive. A soldier got out followed by another, dismounting from the cab. Both had rifles and began walking slowly forward.

"I think we should shoot both of them right now!" hissed Margie.

"Well, hold on honey, let's see what they're gonna do. Maybe they'll just go away, but if they don't, we'll nail them. I think by surprising them we may have a chance. Slowly Donny cocked his gun, with his right hand displaying the Ancestor Brother's Mark on its back.

"What about Lora? How is she gonna live?" asked Betty as she sighted her rifle.

"Well, I guess the Lord will have to get busy, 'cause she ain't got no chance without Him. I hear they kill all the children." Donny paused before saying, "I'll take the one on the right, and you take the one of the left, but wait 'til I give the word."

Margie slowly nodded while carefully aiming.

Chapter 5: A Baby! A Baby!

Donny Stewart slowly tightened his pressure on the trigger while sighting his gun on one of the approaching soldiers.

"Ready?" he asked his wife

"Umm-hmm," she responded quietly as she concentrated on sighting.

Suddenly, from the back of the truck, a little girl came screaming with joy followed by another small girl chasing her. Immediately following them was an older civilian who swept up the first girl. The two soldiers turned, startled by the noise.

From the truck's cab, a young man jumped down, chasing and grabbing the second giggling girl.

"What the…" shouted Donny.

"They're not all soldiers, Donny!"

"Let's not jump to conclusions. Looks to me like they grabbed those children who were trying to escape! I think they're some Goonies." Raising his rifle again, he prepared to fire.

From the truck's cab a woman in a civilian dress, and obviously pregnant, got slowly down meeting the man as he returned with the child.

"Donny! Put down your gun, that girl's pregnant!" she shouted as she undid the window flap and opened it. "You there," she shouted. "What do you want?"

Mary stepped forward, "Just a place to sleep!" she shouted back.

"Put your weapons down!" shouted Donny to the strangers.

Slowly, Harkins and Brunswick lowered their M16s.

"Lay the weapons on the ground!"

After some hesitation and a nod from Mary, they slowly downed their weapons.

"Everybody outta the truck!" Donny shouted from the house.

From the truck's rear, Betty and Roy appeared joining McDee, Tim, Mary, the girls, and the two soldiers. Finally, the nine of them stood waiting and unarmed.

"Stay right there, I'm comin' out!" shouted Donny, then to his wife, "Keep them in your sights and shoot if they make moves for the guns."

Margie nodded while keeping her eyes on the group.

Donny worked on the bolted door, finally removing the plywood and left with his weapon at the ready.

Keeping the group covered, he made his way to the rear of the truck and found it empty.

Addressing the men asked, "So, which one of you speaks for group?"

Mary turned to face him, "I do."

Donny tried to keep his surprise as he moved toward her. "So, who are you all, anyway?"

"We're just traveling and trying to find someplace to rest," answered Mary. As she spoke, she noticed the Mark on Jimmy's hand. She was careful not to display any reaction; however, it was obvious this was not going well.

"Lemme see your hand," instructed Donny.

Slowly, Mary raised her right hand revealing the smooth clear back.

Donny grunted. "What about the rest of you – anybody got the Mark?"

Silence was the answer.

Turning his attention again to Mary be asked, "So, you a bunch of Christians?"

Mary was silent for a moment before answering, "We are."

Donny smiled, "Well, so are we – praise God."

For a moment Mary was stunned, then smiled and turned to the others "They're Christians!" she shouted with a smile.

Donny turned towards the house, "They're Christians, honey. They're Christians!"

32

Twenty minutes later all but Harkins and Brunswick, who said they would take a walk around the house to get a lay of land, were gathered at the kitchen table. Lora was helping her grandmother with coffee cups while Donny got up to unhinge slats in the windows, allowing the fading sunlight inside.

Margie smiled at Mary, "For a second there I thought you was Goonies – they're the worst."

"Yes, we had some encounters with them at our old camp. They seem to enjoy killing and worse."

Mary waited until the coffee was served before approaching Donny with the most important question. "I see," she began feeling awkward, "you have the Mark. You said you were a Christian, but obviously you aren't."

"Oh, don't pay any attention to that," said Margie. "I told the ol' fool not to get it, but out the door he went anyway."

"I had no choice," said Donny. "If you want to buy food, get gas – or whatever – you needed the stupid Mark. I have two people here I love and I'm not gonna let them starve to death or go without electricity and all. I know, I know, I'm going to hell, don't care. My family is worth it."

Mary exchanged glances with Donny. "Let me ask you this, do you love Jesus?"

"I do, and I love God's Word, that's how I know where I'm headed."

"Well, before you start packing your bags for hell, why don't we give Jesus a chance to solve this problem?"

"Well, Preacher, I understand what you're saying, but I don't think there is an exception just for me – and I understand but I don't care. My wife and grandchild eat, they are safe for a while. Knowing I did that for them will be a comfort to me when I die and start roasting hot dogs down under."

"I think we should let that be for now," said Mary. "We have more immediate problems such as this night. We would appreciate it if you would allow us to stay here tonight. Maybe we could sleep in the barn."

33

Margie spoke up. "No, not in the barn – we wouldn't hear of it. Tell me, how far along are you, honey?"

"Well, as close as I can figure, I'm about seven months."

"Yeah, that looks about right. We normally have Lora's bedroom up here, but now you and your hubby can sleep there."

'Preacher if you don't mind we can fix up a cot for you downstairs. That's where we have Lora sleep now in case the Goonies come at night. Mr. and Mrs. Kegler can sleep out here in the living room on the sofa bed."

Returning, both Harkness and Brunswick volunteered to sleep in the barn.

The rest of the night was spent in exchanging stories of how life had changed for each of them. The moon was high before they went to bed.

In the morning, Donny took Tim and Roy out past the barn into the fields, with Scott Brunswick following.

"Used to have lots of crops here, but now we have to hide them. I've let the weeds grow up, but every three feet or so is a row of something that won't grow higher than the weeds. If you look at this from the road it just looks like just a field of weeds, but we are able to get some food from here."

"Wow," said Tim, "This is quite a garden, and very cleverly hidden."

"Yep, I even fix up a basket for the two neighbor ladies down some ways – they are too old."

"Are they Christian?" asked Brunswick.

Donny shrugged his shoulders, "Maybe so, but I really don't know. I knew them before all this, but just to say 'hello' and talk weather. They don't let me too near the house. They don't let anyone near. Nowadays folks just don't know who the trust. 'Sides, I'm afraid to talk religion with anyone."

The three walked in silence for a few seconds before Donny spoke up. "Tell me, Tim, where are you folks headed?"

It was Tim's turn to shrug his shoulders. "We don't really know, or at least, I don't. My wife, Mary, she's sort of the one to look to for directions. The Lord chose her to lead us, you know."

"Chose? How did that happen?"

"Up on the mountain, we had a Prophet."

"A real Prophet?"

Tim nodded. "Yes, sir, if they issued ID cards, his would've said, "Mountain Prophet."

"I'll be. What did he say was going to happen?"

"Well, just about what did. Those alien jerks killed him and his wife."

Donny shook his head, "Imagine that, a real prophet. The closest we come to that was some old man a ways back that lives in the woods. I tried to follow him a couple of times, but lost him. He's sorta a Bible guy that gave us some pretty good advice. He told me about you folks."

"Really, he told you about us?"

"Yes, at least we decided it was you. Just said some of God's people were coming to visit – and I guess that's you. He was real upset when I got the Mark. Said I wouldn't see him anymore, but someone was coming who would know what to do. Haven't seen him since."

"Who was he, what's his name?"

"Don't really know. I asked him once and he said some folks just call him 'Kermit'."

"Kermit? We know him! The kids called him Kermit, but most folks called him the Hermit! He lived in the mountain where the camp was. Everybody talked about him, but never ever saw him – 'til he led us down the mountain to the truck. He was really old, and bent over. He had a cane – more like long branch."

"That's him!"

"Kermit? Hermit?" mused Brunswick, "I never heard of him. Where does he live?"

"No one really knows," said Tim. "I was told he lived in the mountain but that exploded, and now Jim says he saw him near here, so it beats me."

"Maybe we should follow him," suggested Brunswick.

"Oh, people have tried that, but never really found out where he goes."

"Wait 'til I tell Mary!" smiled Tim.

For dinner Betty and Margie prepared a large salad with Margie saying, "We're only able to eat meat now and then – whenever Donny can get some at the market. At first there was plenty of stuff in the market, but now not so much. Most eat what we harvest from the garden."

The veggie dinner was filled with small talk including the news about the Hermit. Mary related about how she was healed from blindness and Tim talked about the girls and how they came to be together. It was approaching midnight before they retired.

Then, a little after two in the morning, Mary nudge Tim.

Tim rolled over still in love with sleep. "Umm?"

"The baby," she whispered. "I think something is happening."

Instantly Tim sat up, all traces of slumber gone. "The baby – you're having the baby?!"

"Hush!" hissed Mary as she groaned as another pain came. "Be quiet don't bother the others it might just be a false alarm."

"Oh my God!" shouted Tim, leaping from the bed and rushing out into the hall. "Baby! Baby! Baby!" he called, rushing from the bedroom and banging on the Stewart's door. He then ran into the living room. "Baby! Baby! The baby's coming!"

Betty was already out of bed, having heard the hammering and yells. She ran to Mary's room with Margie right behind, followed by Tim.

"Wait!" said Betty holding up her hand to Tim. "You wait out here; we'll take care of everything."

"No, not on your life. I wanna be right next to her!"

"Okay, but nothin's gonna happen in the next ten minutes. Why don't you boil us some water – you can be useful that way.

"We'll call you when you can come in."

"Oh yeah, water," said Tim as he rushed into the kitchen and put a pan under the faucet.

A sleepy Roy, finally joining him, sat down heavily at the kitchen table.

"Roy," asked Tim, "why do they need water? I always hear they need it. What do they do with it?"

Roy shrugged his shoulders. "Dunno. But when it boils, I could use a cup of coffee."

Chapter 6: Secret Places

Suddenly the television came to life startling General Valice. "Sterling, get in here!" he shouted.

Sterling rushed back into the general's office to see Abdon's image on the TV.

For a moment Abdon remained silent and unmoving. He was clothed in a dark black robe with a hood. The hood he was wearing shadowed his face so only the tip of his nose was visible. It was difficult to make out the location from where they were broadcasting. Neither Valice nor Sterling recognized what little was visible.

"Greetings," Abdon said finally with his deep less-than-friendly voice. "I bring you greetings from Abaddon our supreme leader. He felt it was necessary to reassure you, our children. The widespread earthquakes you have just witnessed are the first of many natural rumblings of the Earth in preparation for her final death. This was not the so-called Last Day that foolish religious fanatics shout about."

Sterling glanced at General Valice, but the general showed no reaction.

"When we first came we brought to you a warning that this planet would soon die a terrible death. We told you we were here to rescue you from this and bring you into a Forever Tomorrow. What you are seeing now is just the beginning of the Earth's death throes. Many of your friends, family, and fellow humans have died in these earthquakes. Your Earth is going through the death throes. The time grows short."

"You're telling me," mumbled Sterling.

"Shut up!" snapped the General.

Abdon turned and slowly walked to his right until standing in front of a large Earth map easily fifteen feet tall and at least as wide. It showed in detail the entire earth with major cities noted. Located around the map was a series of red circles.

Abdon pointed to one red circle. "The red circles indicate where eruptions have occurred. Some are larger than others, each has had deadly in consequences."

He then pointed to a red circle located in the Antarctic Sea. "Here is where the ships of the brothers and sisters were located. They have all been victims of a large earthquake which occurred on the ocean floor destroying them and their inhabitants. Not only did many of our fellow travelers die, but thousands of your people also perished."

Again, he pointed to the map, this time to the Mediterranean Sea and a point between Cyprus and Israel, west of Lebanon "This is where our mothership has descended, and it houses the magnificent Abaddon. He has come to earth to lead you to the stars." He paused allowing the portent of his words to sink in. "It is from here that he shall speak to you in the coming days, but those days grow short. Make no mistake about it, the days grow short!"

Major Valice turned to Sergeant Sterling. "That's where our Prefect wants me to go!"

Sterling nodded but kept his attention on the screen.

The camera zoomed closer upon the head of Abdon revealing the still shadowed eyes peering out at them.

"I cannot stress enough how important it is for you to cleanse the Earth. The time grows short; the time for caution is at an end. Soon this planet will be destroyed, but we will leave before that happens. Will you? If all religious fanatics are not eliminated before your end comes, no one will escape with us. What I am about to say may sound cruel, but I only say it to save your life and lives of your loved ones. The time for trying to save those who do not have the Mark of Salvation is at an end. It is time to eliminate all – I repeat – all, who do not have this Mark. They must perish. For the sake of your loved ones and your own life, eliminate them without mercy. Mercy times have ended – it is the time of the salvation for your families." Abdon paused considering his next words. "You don't know

39

how much it pains me to talk like this, and we so much want you to live forever in joy and security. But, my children, you must show no mercy to anyone – if there are those in your community who have not received the Mark of Salvation, kill them. It is your duty to mankind! It is your duty to your children! Let tears of regret water the soil of salvation for you and your loved ones!"

With that the screen faded and returned to noisy non-reception.

Sergeant Sterling turned the TV off and both men were silent for a moment.

Finally, General Valice took a take deep breath. "That's what we were just told by the one who visited us earlier. When Captain Bellmore returns, tell him I want him to draft up an order that anyone without the Mark is to be shot on sight – men, woman, and children. Do you understand?" His voice sounded weary, defeated, but determined.

"Yes, sir," replied Sergeant Sterling with enthusiasm.

* * * * *

Before the volcanic eruptions filled the atmosphere, the Alien structure in the Mediterranean could be seen from the shore of Israel. Now, with the presence of the atmospheric ash, very little beyond a few hundred feet could be discerned. Aircraft could no longer land on the pyramid, leaving the only way to and from the structure by boat. As a result, ships were at anchor around the structure swelling the number to hundreds of freighters and passenger vessels. They appeared very small next to the immense towering triangular structures. This structure compared to the former pyramids were gigantic reaching several thousand feet in the air and to unknown depths below – to what depth it descended, no one knew. One day it wasn't there, and the next dawn it towered above the sea with no record of its descent.

How such a structure could descend without detection was the subject of speculation around the globe.

The religious fanatics claimed it didn't descend at all, but rose from the depths of hell. Their claim was that the images which appeared above the earth were satanic images. There never were any 'spaceships' but simply illusions created by the Devil. Of course, no one took them seriously. It was accepted that the unseen descent down to earth was simply another example of the Alien's extreme technology.

Deep beneath the surface level of the pyramid, far from prying eyes, Durk spent his time in the warmth and dark he loved. Here he had real authority, of course not as much as the powerful Abdon or the magnificent Abaddon. He was, however, among the elite in rank. Back on the insufferable Earth, he was surrounded by those dirty animals called humans, and the dreadful adoration of Yahweh. Here he was addressed by his true name and not that dreadful "Durk."

"Honorable One, Hathor, I am here as commanded." The voice came from one of his underlings entering the room. Once again, Durk was reminded of how well he was respected. He loved hearing his new title, 'Hathor The Bull, Servant of Abaddon'. Just the thought brought a smile to his face. So long he had labored under the title of 'Horus the Falcon.'

"Yes, have you prepared my new quarters? Are they ready now?" asked Durk. Now that he had new responsibilities and position, he was entitled to grander quarters

"Yes, most Honorable Hathor, I have seen to its assembly and have included all your wishes. It is ready for you now."

"Very well. You are a good servant."

"Thank you. May I ask a question?"

"Question? Yes."

"Why is the Magnificent Abaddon playing with these human animals? What are they to us? I wonder why he doesn't just eliminate them and assume his rightful command. After all, isn't he in charge of the Word, hasn't he even challenged the revered Yahweh?"

Durk sighed. "Yes, yes – but, well, it's complicated. Their souls are our hostages, but as I said, it's complicated."

"Yes, Honorable Hathor you who know so much more than most of us. We serve."

"Everything was so right when the law was Abaddon's to rule, but times have changed. There are, well, complications."

"Are you talking about..."

"Silence! Do not say His name! Never, never say his name!

"Yes, I understand, I was going to say The Intruder."

"Yes, that's better: The Intruder. That's what he is. If it were not for him, we would now be the rulers of all – oh, the thought of it." Durk lay down and breathed a long slow sigh.

"Now, look what we have to do. I, whose authority extends to all Abdon's kingdom, am forced to parade around Earth as a filthy imposter. I coddle their doubts and fears. I inspire, even praise them when I must. I was told to choose an earthly name I said I wanted it to be 'Dirt' because that's what those creatures are and how I felt being among them. I was told I couldn't be named such, but if I made it Durk they would allow it." He broke into laughter. "So now they pay me homage, they pay dirt homage." Again, he laughed.

"But soon, Honorable Hathor, shall it be over?"

"Patience. First, we must lure as many as possible into our trap where we can hold their souls hostage. Then, we can eliminate all of the filthy beings who refuse by whatever means we choose."

"I have no right to know, Honorable One, but what is the plan? If the Unnamed One, The Intruder, stands at that gate, how do we overcome?"

"This is for the Great Abaddon to know. He has a plan, and he is going to share it with us in his time. I was told this may happen soon."

42

Chapter 7: The New Colonel

Durk got up and preened his body. "Tell me, do I look alright?"

"Yes, of course, Honorable One. You always look wonderful. Many envy you when they see you."

Durk smiled

"Do I have your permission to leave?"

"Go."

Left alone, Durk prepared for the duty ahead. He stood and closed his eyes in preparation for the change, and ugly transformation. Slowly his beautiful form morphed into that of the ugly human again. The process didn't take long, but was uncomfortable. It was as if he put a wet blanket around his beautiful form, giving him the feeling of being suffocated. Picking up his dark cape and putting it around his shoulders, then covered his head with the hood. It was time to go.

As he walked the dark hallways, he could occasionally hear the moans and screams of the vanquished. Their miseries were music to his and other's dark souls. Sometimes he and the others would gather to watch these lost souls agonize. Hearing their pleas for God to rescue them was music to their ears. Their rescue, of course, was the plan – the goal, the hope of all those who Abaddon ruled. For in these conquered godly souls was the rescue of their own; their release from this hell. And, the plan was working so well before 'He', the Unnamed One, The Intruder, came to earth. Now that plan was not so clear. Durk and the others had no choice but to trust that Abdon had a solution, that he kept as a secret, but which would restore him to power, along with others, including himself. Once again Abdon would rule, and he along with the others would be restored to their rightful authorities in heaven.

Durk entered the lift that would take him to the upper level – the Earth level. As soon as the door closed, the elevator began ascending at a great rate, and only began to slow after several minutes had transpired. Finally, a soft whine could be heard as the car slowed until reaching a complete stop. The door opened and Durk was in the familiar narrow corridor that led to one of the main hallways. Exiting, the door closed silently behind, leaving no discernible evidence that it even existed.

Durk walked the hallway leading to the main pedestrian traffic then melded into the stream of humans walking in either direction. Because of who he was, a wide space was accorded him by other fallen angels as he slowly walked to the human elevators for this section. He waited along with others for the first car to open. When it did he walked inside. No one followed, and he journeyed to the fifth floor alone.

When the door opened he exited to his right. Here again there were many humans. Some worked here, others were visitors. Durk hated them all and refused to acknowledge the many bows, salutes, and smiles he received along the way. Finally reaching the Offices of Personnel, he entered without paying attention to the greetings of the female human receptionist.

Walking past several uniformed officers, also ignoring their positions of stiff attention, he continued on.

Once inside the office he was to use that day, he went to the window which looked out and down. In the past, he enjoyed looking out a window so high up. It was as though he was surveying a kingdom, a portion of which was his to rule, but now it was impossible to even see the base below him because of the ash in the air.

Turning, he went to the desk and buzzed the receptionist.

"Yes, sir?" came the human's ugly-sweet voice.

"Send in the first," replied Durk curtly.

Thus, the day began, and promised to be long. One after another hopeful senior officer came in and each Durk found was lacking the characteristics for which he was looking. As far as experience was concerned, all of them had gone through the standard gauntlets required to reach their rank. Some were too friendly, some too relaxed – he was not looking for either. He wanted a hungry officer willing to do anything to get ahead. Durk was not interested in anyone who looked upon the men under his command as his "charges," his children, to be protected and for whom he cared. He wanted a ruthless leader, one willing to sacrifice lives to accomplish goals set out by Durk. The exact kind of officer that would normally be court-martialed – but whom he would cheer.

It wasn't until three in the afternoon that such an officer walked through the door.

He was an Air Force Lt. Colonel. His hat was tucked under his left arm and a file folder in his left hand.

"Sir, Lt. Colonel Dennis Tilly reporting as ordered."

"Let me see the file, Colonel," replied Durk curtly.

Tilly quickly handed over his file, immediately snapping back to attention.

"At ease," muttered Durk as he scanned the file. Finally, Durk looked up at the Air Force uniform to his head, still at attention with eyes focused on some imagined distant object.

"I see you've been in the Air Force for nineteen years."

"Yes, sir."

"I also see you've been passed over for promotion to full bird Colonel twice."

This time there was a slight pause before Tilly answered and when he did it was a less enthusiastic, "Yes, sir."

Durk was silent as he read some more. Finally, he looked at Tilly again. "Seems your superiors think you have a rebel personality. They say you get the job done, but in less than a professional manner. What do they mean by that?"

For a moment some emotion played on Tilly's face as he chose he words carefully. "Sir, I believe in getting the task completed and worry about how pretty I did it later."

Durk nodded. "Yes, I think that's the impression I had."

Durk got up from his chair and went to the side, motioning to Tilly. "Relax. I think we need to talk a little, alien to man, as it were."

"Yes, sir," responded Tilly as his body noticeably breathed out. He followed Durk over to two easy chairs which faced each other with a small coffee table between.

Durk motioned for Tilly to sit, and he did the same. "This religion thing has become a real problem," he began. "I'd like hear your thoughts on that."

Tilly cleared his throat, giving himself time to gather thoughts. "Yes, sir, it's a real problem – but one that would be solved a lot quicker if we weren't so concerned about what people thought." Tilly paused, taking a quick glance to judge the reaction. Seeing Durk nodding, he warmed to the subject.

"Sometimes, sir, I believe the justification and rewards of an operation are not to be judge in the execution of the act but in a hindsight perspective of the good accomplished for the cause or objective."

"Meaning?"

"If I may be blunt, sir?"

"Of course."

"The problem, as I see it, is we're being too namby-pamby about these Christian creeps. Why are we pussyfooting around? Going to the stars with you is the greatest thing that has ever happened on this planet – to mankind, and we are treating it as if it's some kind of evil consequence of getting rid of the religious fanatics."

Durk nodded. "I see from your records that you have been taken off a combat role and placed in charge of administering personnel for the division. Also, I'm aware that if you are passed over for promotion one more time you will be discharged."

Tilly nodded slowly, "Yes, sir."

"I think they may have been mistaken. I think you may very well be the man who I've been looking to make the District Commander of the Fifth District."

"Sir?" was all that Tilly could manage.

"You heard me, and I think a promotion to full bird Colonel would be in order too."

"I... I don't know what to say, sir. It would be my honor and privilege to serve you in that capacity."

"Oh, I don't know if you will think that when you finally take over. I'll be watching you very closely, Colonel, and I will not hesitate to replace you the moment I feel you are not living up to my expectations."

"I understand, sir."

Durk got up from his chair and went to the window, gazing out for a moment in silence before he continued. "Are you aware many of the Christians have fake Marks now, and are hiding among our Chosen?"

"I've heard the rumor, sir."

"The rumor is true. One day we knew who they were and where they were. The next day they disappeared – obviously living among the Chosen. This makes the identification of these dirty Christians much more difficult. Have you any thoughts on how we can route them out?"

"To my way of thinking we have to be less discerning in identification procedures," Tilly suggested.

"Meaning?"

"Kill anyone you think might possibly be a Christian whether they have the Mark or not." Tilly then held up his hand. "Before you judge me as being cruel, sir, let me explain. If there are, say five million people and we killed two million because we think they might possibly be one of the Religious Fanatics, and say we are wrong about a third of them. By sacrificing those lives we are saving three million. I'm sorry, but I will take that math. I would rather have three million thank me in future than delay so long that no one is saved."

Durk's lips moved but whether it was into a smile or grimace was difficult to tell. "You're going to have a problem the troops. While you may see the validity of the action, your troops may not. We find that many of the troops are extremely slow to take action, or in some cases absolutely refuse. There are reports of some desertions."

Tilly nodded. "Being associated with the Personnel Records I'm aware of the desertions, of course. But here is my view, and sir I will be absolutely honest. I hope you will not hold it against me. The men under my command must be treated no different than the civilians they are judging. If a soldier is slow to perform, he is publicly executed – no different than we do civilians. I assure you once the troops see the penalty for hesitation they will step up their game," he smiled.

Durk nodded. "I believe you are right."

"As for the desertions, I have two solutions. The first is obvious, any caught are immediately shot; however, I think we should set guards at night around all military installations. The guards are told to shoot on sight anyone, and I mean anyone, trying to leave the camp, base, or airfield without written permission. The whole purpose of all these harsh measures is to reinforce our demand upon the troops on their missions, and the penalties for failure."

"Yes, Colonel, and I hope you will keep the same in mind for yourself. Welcome to District 5, Colonel."

Chapter 8: New Tears

As they drove, both McDee and Harkins saw burned houses and stores, most with their possessions or inventories scattered about, evidence of visits by Goonies.

"That's the group we have to avoid," said McDee. "The Visitor's soldiers are bad enough, but those Goonies are worse – burning after plundering just because they enjoy it."

Harkins nodded, keeping his eyes on the road. "Yeah, not to mention cutting off hands. I've heard sometimes they don't kill the person before taking the hands."

"Slow down, I see a sign," said McDee. He studied the highway sign. "It says to turn left here for the lake. I'm pretty sure Camp Adam is that way," he said looking at the surrounding scene and checking his map. "It's been a couple of years since I was here, and then it was at night, but I'm pretty sure Stephanie drove down this road." He looked at the map again. "Yeah, and then Route 143 goes by Santeetiah Lake. From there, we took a little dirt road, but I don't remember where it is exactly. We'll just have to keep our eyes open."

Harkins mumbled his agreement as he turned the wheel. "Yeah, I know," he said, "I'm glad you thought about doing this. Sitting around and listening to a baby being born isn't my idea of fun."

McDee nodded. "Well, I thought about staying there but looked like the ladies had it in hand."

They drove on in silence for an hour without passing another vehicle. Finally, Reverend McDee spotted a sign announcing the next crossroad was Highway 143.

Approaching it, they spotted a combination grocery store and gas station. It was a typical stand-alone wood building with a couple of pumps in front. It showed no sign of being anything other than what it advertised. There was a big sign posted in one of the large picture windows: No Mark – No Service. These days this was a typical sign, and posted by store owners who would not give service to Christians. Not having such a sign would bring a visit by some Goonies to the store. But it wasn't the sign that disturbed the Reverend. It was the police car parked in the side lot. The markings showed it was a North Carolina State Trooper.

"Don't do anything out of the ordinary, just turn down 143 and keep going," whispered McDee.

As they made the turn and started down the new road, Harkins checked his rear-view mirror.

"Oh, no," he whispered. "He's coming."

"Well, let's not jump the gun here. He may just be going down this road for some other reason. You got your ID card?"

"Yep," answered Harkins just as the police car's lights turned on.

Immediately Harkins pulled over and waited for the state trooper to approach. Harkins could see he was alone in the squad car.

He noticed Reverend McDee reaching under the seat where he'd stashed his gun, making sure it was handy.

The trooper approached slowly, casually putting a hand on his side-arm while stopping at the rear side window and peering inside. Satisfied there were only two, he approached the driver's side window. "You got your license and ID?" he asked with a professional tone.

Jim was ready and held up both documents which the trooper took in his gloved hand.

"So, we have an Army boy here," the trooper said gruffly. "Lemme see your hand."

"Why is that necessary – you can see my ID."

"Shut up and show me your hand!"

Harkins slowly held up his hand.

"No Mark," said the trooper with some amazement in his voice while drawing his sidearm. "I heard some scuttlebutt about a bunch of army boys deserting. Looks like I have me one right here." He then turned towards McDee. "What about you?"

McDee held up his hand.

Again, the trooper grunted. "So, you're both Christians."

"Yes, sir."

"Tell me," he asked, looking at Harkins "what's the story? Why you Christians driving around? You know that's against the law. We got orders to kill you on site, and anybody helping you," he said, raising his gun.

"So, that's it?" challenged Harkins. "You–"

"Sit up!" shouted the trooper as he saw Reverend McDee lean forward. "Got something under the seat? Put your hands behind your head. You make one move and I'll shoot you – I should have already!"

McDee remained silent, but sat up while slowly putting his hands behind his head and interlocking his fingers. The officer didn't tell him he needed to do that, but he'd seen enough cop shows to know that's what they wanted.

The trooper turned his attention back to Harkins, but before he could speak, Harkins began talking.

"Is this police enforcement nowadays? Go around shooting people for no reason but that Mark? Well, I got something to tell you Buster – I'm a Christian, so go ahead shoot me; I'll see you in hell!" This last was delivered with all the venom could muster.

"Shut up before you attract some attention!" hissed the trooper, looking around as he holstered his weapon. "My name is Thorman – David Thorman. I'm a Christian, too."

"Wha..." exclaimed Harkins as he looked at McDee to see the same bewildered look as his own. "Have you got the Mark?"

Trooper Thorman nodded. "I do."

"I thought once you got the mark it meant you didn't believe."

Thorman nodded. "And, I didn't. I went to get the Mark just like everyone else. In fact, maybe part of it was I couldn't stay a State Trooper unless I did. I don't know. What are you boys up to tonight?"

"Ever hear of Camp Adam?" asked Reverend McDee.

Trooper Thorman smiled. "Yes, it used to be just up this road."

"Used to be?"

Thorman nodded. "All the Christians left months ago. They were arrested."

The Reverend and Harkins exchanged glances.

"Now, first I need some info about you two."

"Like what?"

"Well, you can start by telling me where you're from."

Reverend McDee leaned forward, "Well, originally I lived in Camp Noah – ever hear about that?"

"Camp Noah! Yes, Old Camp Adam was founded by some people from there. You know the Prophet?"

"Yes, I knew him very well. Did you hear he was executed and that Camp Noah disappeared in a volcano eruption? I believe everybody in the camp died except me and a few others that escaped."

"Heard about The Prophet. We knew the mountain erupted and there was talk that everyone in the camp died – at least was the story, but I hear they just couldn't find them."

Thorman turned his attention to Harkins. "What's your story?"

Harkins explained how he was slated for execution because he didn't have the Mark but a buddy of his named Brunswick saved him and they both escaped. "He's in the same boat as you. He was forced to get the Mark, but doesn't believe in the Brother crap."

"Maybe it will make your friend feel a little better to know everybody at Camp New Adam has the Mark. We all have it.

"Oh my God!" said Harkins smiling. "He'll be happy to hear that."

"So, what happened to the people at Camp Adam? I was under the impression there were between 150 and 200 people," said McDee.

Thorman shook his head. "After my family became Christians we came here looking for the camp. I was familiar with the name and I knew the location. When we got here, they were all gone. Where they went we don't know. At first, we thought they might be hiding in forest, but later heard they had escaped. Where they're now is anybody's guess. The rumor is they have put the Mark on themselves in order to blend in with everyone else."

Revered McDee shook his head, "I don't think that's what happened."

The Trooper looked up and down the road. "You follow me, and I'll take you to the new camp."

Thorman got into his squad car and began driving down the road. They passed by the Bay of Lake Santeetiah. South of the lake, they came to the gravel road which led to the old Camp Adam, but the Trooper did not go down the road. Instead, he followed the curve to the left and continued down the road leading to some foothills. The road was in terrible condition – later, the Trooper would explain that it was on purpose. Potholes were so deep they had to slowly drive off the road around them. He and others from the New Camp Adam had dug them to discourage visitors.

"When it rains this road must be a nightmare," said Harkins, shaking his head.

Finally, there was a sign reading "Santeetiah Forest Station."

Trooper Thorman parked his car in front of the station, but motioned Harkins to park in front of a large garage that sat at right angles to the Station. The garage had a width of three or four cars, but the length was easily five or six car lengths deep.

53

Going to the second garage door, he opened it and motioned Harkin to park their truck inside. Thorman then opened another garage door and parked his squad car next to them.

Harkins was about to shut off the truck when Trooper Thorman shouted, "Keep it running!" as he closed both garage doors. He then went to the left side wall where he lifted a panel then pressed a button. At first it looked like the entire wall began to slide sideways, but turned out to be only half, which was a door-wall, hung on hidden rollers above. Harkins and the Reverend saw a hidden a tunnel leading forward and down.

Walking over to them, the trooper smiled, "Okay. Let's introduce you to Camp New Adam," he said as he climbed into the back.

"One thing that's nice is that we are out of the dirty air – I mean, all that volcanic ash that keeps on coming down," said Thorman "From what I hear there were almost sixty volcanoes that erupted around the world. That ash is circulating around the globe and eventually heading this way."

"I didn't think there were that many volcanoes in the world!" said Harkins.

Thorman smiled. "I studied a little geology in college. How many dormant and active volcanoes do you think are in the USA?"

Harkins thought for a moment. "Well, 'course we know about Cloud Mountain, and I know there are a couple in the Rockies – and I'll throw a few more in there that I probably don't know about – I guess about nine."

Thorman smiled. "In the US, there are one hundred and sixty."

"One hundred and sixty! That doesn't seem possible!"

"There are almost five hundred around the world. Now the point is, the information we receive at the station is that many them erupted at the same time. The immediate disaster from the eruptions killed millions; however; there are longer-term consequences from all that volcanic ash in the air. The release of the ash in the air will mean a decrease in the sun's rays reaching us. I think we are in for some chilly days, not to mention the difficulty in breathing."

"How will that affect you folks down here?"

"Well, we're hoping we can make it through. We're working on a way to provide heat. I think the walls and the surrounding earth are good insulators, but we need some heat. In addition, we're developing ways to filter the air."

The square walls of the garage gave way to cement walls that curved at the top as they drove down. There were three tunnels each at least one hundred yards in diameter leading away from a cavernous common area measuring at five hundred feet or more. In this huge area several trucks were parked, now including their own.

"Unbelievable," said Reverend McDee.

* * * * *

Mary was losing energy. Tim had talked his way into the room and was at her side, occasionally offering cold water and loving touches as she struggled through her labor.

"How you doin' honey?"

Mary closed her eyes. "I used to think labor would be joyful," she smiled. "But I've changed my mind."

"What's my license number?" Tim asked.

"Huh? Your license number! Are you crazy? I'm in the middle of having a baby and you want to know your license number!"

"Well," smiled Tim, "You're the one who said you could remember it forever."

"You're nuts!" snapped Mary. A contraction came, and Tim watched as she tightened preparing to push. The push brought from her a growling sound. Finally, the pressure eased and she fell back on the bed exhausted.

Tim took a washcloth and cooled her face. Suddenly, Mary grabbed Tim's hand.

"C630887777086!" She snapped, with a sound that could be a laugh. "Oh, how long is this going to last! I want my baby now!"

"Hang in there, honey," encouraged Betty Kegler. "We can't rush these babies. They come when they're ready and not before."

"Yes, honey, just try to relax," encouraged Tim.

"It's really amazing how husbands can be so patient and philosophical when they don't have a body inside trying to rip them apart!" laughed Betty.

"What time is it?" asked Mary.

"It's going on eleven o'clock."

"What's going on with the ash cloud – is it getting near?"

"No, just seems to hang there. There is no wind right now."

"Are the Reverend and Harkins back yet?"

"Not yet – now never mind about all of that," said Tim. "You've got a job here that needs all of your attention. We'll take care of the other stuff."

* * * * *

Harkins and McDee got out of the truck and began walking with Thorman in the huge, enclosed area. The area was so large, and combined with the roundness of the walls, that it prevented echoes.

"What is this place?" asked McDee in wonder.

"It was supposed to be a huge water tunnel from the mountains east of here and was to run down to Charlotte then further before splitting with half going south and the other half going north. Ever hear of the huge Moffat Water Tunnel in Colorado?"

"No," smiled Harkins, "Water tunnels aren't a favorite past time of mine."

"Well, it's just about the biggest one, up 'til this one. This one is many times bigger, but they never got further than this. When those Aliens, or whatever came, everybody started walking off construction jobs and this one was no different. I guess they figured they were headed for the stars so, why build anything?"

Thorman turned, pointing down one of the tunnels. "Each of these tunnels runs from ten to fifty miles into the hills," he smiled. "I wouldn't be surprised if we could put ten thousand people in here – course that's if we fix it up."

"You obviously have power."

"Yeah, the east tunnel was the one they were working on when those space jockeys showed up. And it wasn't long before the workers left. I guess they were hoping to hop on a spaceship. But no one ever turned off the power. I think most of the power places are running on automatic and probably, as time goes on, one by one they'll just stop. I don't think many people are working at power stations – or, anywhere else for that matter."

"How many people are here now?"

"We got close to a hundred – every one of them has that Mark."

"So, let me make sure I understand this, you all have the Mark, but all of you have decided you don't want it anymore.

"Exactly," said Thorman.

"And all of you want to be Christians?"

"Well, that's what they've said. We sure don't want to be part of those demons – and that's what we all think that's what they are."

Thorman put his hands on his hips and leaned forward.

"I'll tell you this," he began. "Everyone here believes there's a God, and what's happening is evil."

Reverend McDee turned to Harkins. "I think this would be a great place for us to come." Harkins nodded

Turning to Thorman, McDee asked, "Do you think they would let us come here? There are nine of us."

Thorman smiled, "I can guarantee you they would be overjoyed if you came here. Obviously, you don't have the Mark. You'd be the only people like that. Tell you the truth, it would give the rest of us hope knowing God brought us some unmarked Christians to live among us – and teach us."

"Well, we'll go back to our folks and see what they say. Can you show us around a little?"

Thorman turned motioning Harkins and McDee to follow. The slope leveled out making the walk comfortable. As they approached the lit tunnel, several people turned out to meet them. Harkins and McDee both felt they were being scrutinized as they approached.

"Friends, I've got some people here for you to meet. And the amazing thing is that Reverend McDee and Sergeant Harkins here are unmarked Christians!"

* * * * *

There were no clouds that night, and the absence of the moon made the stars seem even brighter. It was a rare, clear night, one meant for quiet thoughts, tender kisses, and maybe birthing babies. The only sounds disturbing the lovely night were Mary's occasional screams.

As the night grew older, the contractions were drawing ever closer, and though she knew each contraction brought her sweet baby nearer, she was tiring fast. Mary's delivery brought sweat to her face, as each new periodic contraction seemed to last forever. Her initial joy was replaced by a weariness, which she silently begged would end.

Tim held his wife's hand and the anguish was written on his face, emphasized by the occasional tear escaping his eye.

"Good, honey. Good. You're doing really good, baby." He would repeat. His glances to the women in the room pleaded for them get the baby out.

It was almost three in the morning before the women shooed Tim out of the room in preparation for the final push.

"Now, you just go out there and wait – if you want something to do, make sure the water's still hot – and you can always say a few prayers."

Ten minutes later came the final couple of pushes and mother's moans.

"Okay, honey," encouraged Betty, "just one more. I think one more is all we need."

Again, Mary groaned with effort as she and nature tried to force the baby into this world. Finally, Mary felt the baby leave. She couldn't help throwing her sweaty face back and give an exhausted joyful laugh.

Betty grabbed the baby and cut the umbilical cord. She had some training with birthing babies in the past, and immediately tilted the baby to drain any water in the lungs.

"It's a baby girl! It's a girl!" shouted Nora.

Betty held the baby while patting its back. Then, laying the baby on the bed breathed into the baby's mouth encouraging a first breath.

There were no clouds that night, and the absence of the moon made the stars seem even brighter. It was a rare, clear night, one meant for quiet thoughts, tender kisses, and maybe birthing babies. The only sounds disturbing the lovely night were Mary's occasional screams when that first breath never came.

Chapter 9: Discovered

"So, how long have you folks been living here?" asked Harkins.

"Well," began Trooper Thorman, "we knew about these tunnels for a long time – in fact, some of the folk around here were working in them. About a year ago, we decided we needed a new place to live – a safe place. It was getting too dangerous where we were. Too many people starting to look for Marks, and some friends we'd known for years started noticing that we were different. They knew we had the Mark, but we weren't jumping up and down with joy for the Visitors. We knew it would only be a matter of time before they put it together. Plus, there was a rumor that some Christians were hiding in plain site with fake marks on their hands."

"We were meeting secretly in each other's homes, but were afraid the neighbors would notice the cars and start asking questions. Of course, we tried other things. For a while we even advertised a dance and we would secretly meet before and after, but it got kind of iffy. Finally, we decided to make the big move. One of our church members worked on the water tunnel project and knew it was abandoned, so we moved in."

Reverend McDee nodded. "Well, I think the Lord led you to the right place. Yes, I've been around the Marked enough know it isn't only the absence of the Mark that clues them into who of us are Jesus Freaks, it's how we talk – and don't talk. Our behavior in general clues them in to us."

"Exactly," said Thorman. "The tunnel has provided real security, and was large enough for living arrangements." He went on to explain that the width of the tunnel allowed for apartment-like structures to be built against one side, with plenty of room left for people to walk and drive the golf carts that they appropriated from abandoned golf courses.

Each apartment's outside wall was the connecting wall to the next apartment in one long line of connected structures. Some apartments were two stories tall, and one was even three.

"So where did all of this building material come from?" Harkins asked.

"Lots of abandoned lumber yards around," replied Thorman. "Nobody is building anything these days. We're just able to help ourselves." Pausing, he smiled, "At one of the lumber yards we ran into some trouble. I was helping to load some two-by-fours, when this fellow pops up with a shotgun. He was madder than a hornet and I thought he was gonna shoot us. I apologized, telling him who we were, and why we needed the lumber. To this day, I don't know why I told him all that but, well, wouldn't you know, turns out this fella is a Christian and now he lives here with his family. In fact, that three-story there is his. We all tell him he's just trying to show off," laughed Thorman.

Reverend McDee shook his head. "Doesn't that beat all – I tell you, the way God works just amazes me all the time," he smiled.

"So how many folks you got?" asked Thorman.

"Well, as I said, counting the children, we have nine."

"I'm hoping you all decide to join us here. We could construct a couple more homes – real nice ones – in no time. We got some pretty talented people here."

Finally, they bid each other goodbye with McDee promising to visit again. Outside, the early winter temperature made them button up. Reaching the highway, Reverend McDee turned to Harkins. "So, what do you think about joining them?"

Reverend nodded. "I'm for it, but we'll talk about it when we get back home. Right now, I got a little baby on my mind that I wanna see."

"Just as long as I don't have to change diapers," smiled Harkins.

* * * * *

The ash in the air was not as bad as it had been. To the west, the setting sun was able to peak through with a promise of brighter days ahead, though that wasn't the forecast. The winter months were upon them and the cold was reflected in the farmhouse. On the farm, the darkness had moved inside hearts as the group quietly gathered outside.

Tim carried the small box made with spare wood put together with more tears than nails. There were no hymns, no weeping – just the quiet crunching of fall leaves beneath their feet as they followed Tim.

He and Betty selected the site just up the hill in back of the farmhouse beneath a young pine. Tim insisted on digging the grave alone. He grabbed the shovel and without a word dug while others watched from the house. In fact, Tim had been silent since the baby's death, only issuing occasional grunts. As he finished digging, he motioned for the others to join him.

Slowly Tim lowered the box into the grave. Muffled grief could be heard coming from the women with Mary finally breaking down.

Finally, Tim stood up. "I would appreciate it if no words were said over the grave. I think we all can say silent goodbyes."

There was no objection to this father's request and the only sounds continued to be the muffled sobs. Then, one by one, each turned and walked to the house leaving only Mary, Tim, and the two girls, standing at the grave. They stood silently for a long time. Wordlessly, Mary turned and left with the girls. Tim stayed behind and covered the grave. Finishing, he walked slowly to the house where he quietly sat alone and the others allowed him his space.

The hours following were quiet ones until broken by the sound of Harkin's truck pulling into the drive. A few minutes later Harkins and McDee entered the house and immediately were struck by the silence.

"What's going on?" asked Harkins.

Quietly, Betty Kegler brought him up to date. McDee was stunned hearing Betty tell of the tragedy, while he stared at the closed bedroom door. Finally, McDee went to Mary's bedroom door and opened it slowly. She was lying on the bed staring at the ceiling. "May I come in?" he asked softly.

Mary raised her hand silently motioning him to come.

Reverend McDee sat on the bed and held her hand as Mary looked at him with a face on the edge of tears.

"Mary, there are no words I can say that will ease your grief or explain your baby's passing. But know that we all are shedding tears. When you are ready, we'll talk. If you don't mind, could I say a prayer that God will comfort you?"

Mary nodded slowly.

McDee then folded his hands over Mary's and prayed.

As Reverend McDee came out of the bedroom Donny asked, "How's she doing?"

McDee's look at Donny was all the reply he needed to make. Sitting down at the kitchen table, Reverend McDee took a breath and exhaling slowly. "It'll take time, but she'll be alright."

"Should I go in to her?" asked Margie.

"No. I think she needs some alone time with her husband. Where is he?"

"I saw him go outside."

McDee got up and went out the door. He spotted Tim sitting on the ground near the baby's grave. He was leaning against the nearby tree with his head against the bark, eyes closed.

McDee made his way over to him, stopping a few feet away.

Tim opened his eyes, and then closed them again. "Go away. I don't wanna hear your God trash."

McDee did not respond, nor did he move. Finally, Tim opened his eyes again. "Did you hear me, old man? Get the hell away. I don't want anything to do with you or your lousy God – He's a baby-killer!" Suddenly, Tim stood up with clenched fists.

McDee's expression did not change, nor did he move.

"I'll tell you about your God, old man. He doesn't care about us, we're his entertainment! Right now, he's probably rolling around and laughing at me and Mary." These last words had venom in them. "You almost sucked me in – yes, you did. 'Know God is real', oh, I know that alright. I just got fooled about him by you. I bought into the loving kindness bit, stories about how he wants to love us – it's all bullshit, damn you, it's all bullshit…"

Unable to finish, he began to sob silently.

McDee moved to him, wrapping his arms around him.

"Damn you, McDee," sobbed Tim.

For several moments, the two men stood as Tim's tears poured out his grief on McDee's shoulder. Finally, McDee stepped back but kept his hand on Tim's shoulder. "Can I talk now? Will you hear me?"

Tim nodded as he wiped his eyes.

"Tim, you're asking the question every human being has asked since the beginning: 'Why?' There are so many tragedies in the world, and people raise their hands to God and ask, 'Why?' The answers to that question may never be answered while we live. We are not on a journey where there's a formula we can use to divine God's motives or Satan's strategies. It isn't ours to figure out all mysteries. Our job is to believe The Almighty has done that already. It would make our lives a lot easier, I suppose, if we knew the ultimate reasons for every good and bad thing that we experience. However, our life on earth is not a fact-finding journey: it's a faith-finding journey."

"Faith," repeated Tim with a hint of disgust. "I don't want faith, I want my baby."

"I know. When my wife died, I think my tears were more for me than her – I wanted her back, beside me. I wanted to hear her laughter and feel her loving touches and quiet hugs. But she was gone, and why? I didn't know then, don't know now, nor will I until the hereafter. I must trust God knows. I also trust that He has his arms around my loved ones now and they will be waiting for me in the time to come. That's what faith is – trusting God."

"I don't know if I can ever trust Him again."

"Nobody expects you to heal instantly, not even God. It takes time. There are no words I can say that have the soothing balm your soul so desperately needs. Grief is a season, not a day. Some grief lasts for only days, others for years. I think the deepest griefs are with us until we die. We just bury our tears under stuff we use to fill those spaces in our lives, and only now and then do we let them out. Don't let anyone tell you that time will heal all. For some, our grief-time doesn't do much. For some, their grief is just plastered over and we hide from its sorrow. For others, time allows our faith to rise and provide comfort. But we need time to grieve within ourselves, and for ourselves. For this we just need time. Once we have that time, we are able to allow God's spirit to comfort us. We need to allow His Spirit to work within us. It all takes time, Tim. But I'll tell you what doesn't take time – start to concentrate on someone other than yourself. I don't wanna sound mean, but you're out here feeling sorry for yourself, while your wife, a mother-in-grief, lays alone in bed in that house! It's time you started thinking about her and not yourself. You need to get in there and comfort her – and not only her, but those two little girls need you right now, too."

Tim looked at McDee as if suddenly discovering a truth. Without a word, he began running into the house. Inside he didn't pay attention to anyone but grabbed Alison and Katie and knelt holding them to him, and the three shed their tears.

Finally pulling back, said, "Let's go in the bedroom," Holding hands they opened and closed the door and went to Mary lying on her side with the blanket drawn up over her head. Mary turned and held out her arms as desperate tears began to flow from them all.

* * * * *

In the following weeks, the temperature continued to drop as the ash in the air brought an early winter. Once the snow fell, Donny told them they could no longer venture out around the house, or even leave. The snow tracks would be a dead giveaway to roaming Goonies that someone was living there.

However, when they did have to leave the house, they went out the back door, making sure their tracks to the barn were kept as few as possible and narrow in width, hidden from view of the road. From the barn, they could reach the harvest of the garden's crop. There were a few instances when they were alerted to someone passing on the road, but none stopped, at least so far.

The winter months passed slowly, but eventually yielded to spring. With spring came new hope, not only for the others but also for Mary.

They had not journeyed back to the tunnels for fear their tracks would lead someone to the farm, or tunnel; however, now that the spring was here, Reverend McDee approached Mary.

"If you feel up to it, I would like to take you to the tunnels. I think it might be a good place for us."

"Yes, I've thought about them," said Mary. "Hopefully the Goonies have not found out about them."

Before Mary could approach the group, it was Betty who brought it up. "Sergeant Harkins," began Betty, "tell us again about this camp you found."

Sergeant Brunswick looked up, his immediate interest peaked. "Yeah, how many people are there?"

Harkins shrugged shoulders. "I don't know exactly, but I think they said about a hundred, maybe a little less."

"Roy and I were talking about it," said McDee, "and now that spring is here, maybe it's time for us to go there. We don't know how much longer the Goonies will pass here without coming in."

"Yes, no doubt it would be safer than this," said Harkins. Turning to Margie, he asked her how she felt.

Margie was silent for a moment. "Well, honey," she said, looking at Donny, "I don't think I want to move. This is our home. We had our children here and we grew old here. This is the home our little Lora knows. I don't think I could live anywhere else."

Donny smiled. "I feel the same way. When my life ends, I think this is the place where it should happen. I guess I'm old enough now that I'm ready to meet our Lord when He wants, and I hope He wants it to be here. However..."

"But," interrupted Margie, "it's Lora's future we should be thinking about."

Donny nodded. "Yeah, her whole life is ahead of her – whatever that means these days."

"I hate that she has to sleep in the basement. What kind of childhood is that?"

Harkins spoke up. "I saw a girl there that looked about the same age as Lora."

"Well, I think we should put it on hold for a while. I think for now we are safe here, and everything we need is available. As Donny and Margie don't mind us staying here, so I think we should stay put for the time being."

Chapter 10: Recovery

Summer was finally coming, but the temperatures were not as expected. While there were days when the skies cleared, and temperatures reached close to seventy, they normally hovered ten degrees below, nearing only sixty.

Sergeant Sterling knocked on Captain Bellmore's door, and not waiting for a reply, opened it. Bellmore looked up from paperwork, annoyed by the sudden intrusion. Sterling gave a perfunctory salute wishing it was General Valice. He wanted General Valice to receive the credit that might come from this news, but he was temporarily at the pyramid.

"Sir, Intelligence just forwarded information that a mole within a group of Christians has contacted us and given the location where they are hiding."

Bellmore jumped up so fast his chair rolled back hitting the wall. "Great! Some Christians at last!"

"Yes, sir," smiled Sterling, "the field commandeer is asking for clearance to execute them when he captures them in accordance with the edict."

"Humph," said Bellmore, his usual sound when he started thinking. Walking around his desk, the Captain rested against the front. "Contact them and tell them not to kill these Christians. If they ask why, tell them we need to show our people these Christian types aren't in some secret location singing God songs. Second, these Christians probably know where some more of their kind might be hiding."

"From what I understand, they don't rat out other Christians," said Sterling

"Oh, that's because the right persuasions haven't been used," Bellmore smiled. "Okay. Get moving Sterling, I want our troops on the road within the hour."

Smiling to himself, Bellmore fantasized that when the Christians were captured, it could easily mean a promotion.

* * * * *

Mary came into the dining room of the farmhouse with Tim and the girls. Tim was holding Mary's hand and the look on his face showed they clearly had something on their minds. Those in the kitchen were silent, anticipating what the couple had to say.

Tim cleared his throat. "Mary and I have been talking and I want you all to know something," he said in a tight voice. "Don't look for me to go around singing God's praises. I've told Mary this and I wanted to tell you too. Don't try to talk me back being a good-boy Christian, it ain't gonna happen. But I will support my wife, who I love beyond measure, and I will do anything I can to help all of you."

For a moment, silence hung over the room.

Finally, Brunswick asked, "So Mary, how do you feel about that?"

"I feel Tim is entitled to his own beliefs, or non-beliefs," responded Mary, then focusing on Brunswick, "Tell me, Sergeant Brunswick, how do you feel?"

"Me? Well, I ahh – I feel fine."

Mary continued to look at Brunswick then turned to Sergeant Harkins. "Tell us more about this cave you visited. Reverend McDee says it's a group of Christians."

"Yes, it's phenomenal!" answered Harkins.

"Where is it?" asked Brunswick.

"Hold off on that Scott," interrupted Mary. "I want to know if you had a chance to examine their hands."

"I did – they all have the mark, but say they've now become Christians."

"So, they're traitors to the Aliens and now are Christians? How do you know they won't betray us?" asked Brunswick.

"I don't," replied Harkins. "The question I keep asking myself is: 'Is that possible?'"

Mary touched Harkins' arm. "In the Bible, it says that Christ went into the bowels of hell for his people. If Christ is willing to do that for dead souls, I think he's willing to seek out those with the mark. I think He looks at souls and not marks. Perhaps He's waiting for someone to remove the mark from them."

"Remove? Did you say remove?" asked Donny.

"Yes, Donny," she said smiling and motioning him to come to her. "I know a man, known by many as The Prophet, who does it in the name of Christ. I've come to believe one of God's purposes for my being here may be removal of the Mark."

Cautiously, Donny Stewart approached Mary, who took his hand and held it between hers. Closing her eyes, she was quiet for several moments. Donny looked at his wife in bewilderment. Finally, Mary opened her eyes and smiled.

"Jim Stewart. Do you love Jesus Christ?"

"I do."

"Do you believe that He is the Savior of mankind sent to redeem us to God the Father?"

Donny nodded, "Yes, I do."

Slowly, Mary removed her hands. Looking down at his right hand, Donny saw it was unblemished as a baby boy.

Donny let out a whoop, and Nora joined him while the others clapped.

"I thought I was a goner!" shouted Donny.

Mary watched and waited while the others enjoyed the moment. Even Tim was smiling and clapping. After several minutes, the group quieted down.

"That's the happy news of the day," said Mary gaining everyone's attention, "Now comes the bad news: Soon, we will prisoners, but fear not. God is with us. Be patient. Offer no resistance; trust that the Lord has a plan."

70

Chapter 11: They're Coming

Sergeant Sterling answered the phone impatiently. With the General gone it seemed everyone was making demands upon him. "Yes? What is it?" he snapped.

"Sergeant, this is Captain Bellmore. I am with a Christian I found standing by the road. I'm sending him to you. I want him in jail until I return."

"Really? Yes, sir, I'll be waiting. He was standing by the road?"

"Yes, just found him standing next to the road like he was waiting."

"Sounds like a nut case, but then aren't they all?"

"Well, no matter as long as he doesn't have the Mark, he's another one we can use to prove not all those crazies have one. Oh, contact the TV station and tell them to stand by when I return. They can interview me and film the prisoners. I want this one, and the ones I bring in, to be on the tube. This nut even confirmed the information we received about some more Christians just down the road. I'm headed there now."

Forty-five minutes later a Corporal came into Sterling's office announcing they were bringing in the prisoner. "This guy is old, I mean, ancient," he added.

The door opened, and the prisoner entered, escorted by two soldiers. He wasn't in cuffs.

Sergeant Sterling examined the old man silently before asking, "How old are you?"

"Well, tell you, I just lost count."

"Lemme see your hand," instructed Sterling. He looked at the hand so creased by age it was difficult to see whether there was a mark or not. However, Valice eventually was satisfied that there was no mark. "So, what's your name?"

"Well, lately I've been known by some as Kermit."

"Kermit, where are your people?"

71

"Oh, they're everywhere."

"Ah-ha – I knew it!" exclaimed Sterling.

"Now, old man – er, Kermit, can you tell me where we can find some so we may help them?"

"Well, most of them you can't get to – at least now."

"What do you mean?"

"Just what I said. But I did tell your Captain where some Christians are living, but he knew about them already."

"I want to know about others. So, I'll ask you one more time, where are they?"

"Oh, from what I understand they are all over, but thanks to you not as many."

"Put him in the stockade," snapped Sterling. "Hold him there for Captain Bellmore."

"Yes, sir."

Oh, Sergeant Sterling," said the Hermit, "don't you want to know why I came, or I should say, was brought here?"

Sterling looked at the old man. "What are you talking about?"

"I came to advise you not to harm these Christians when you take them into custody – your life depends upon it." The Hermit's voice was low, not belligerent, but had the tone of one concerned.

"How dare you speak to me like this! And how did you know my name?"

The Hermit smiled, though his wrinkles concealed it. "Oh, I've known you quite a while, David."

Turning to the soldiers, Sterling snapped "Take this wrinkled jerk away!"

* * * * *

There was a chill in the air, so Mary put a blanket around herself for the walk up to the grave. She sat there not really thinking nor feeling anything. It was simply peaceful to sit next to the grave.

Approaching footsteps startled her and looking up, she saw the Reverend McDee.

"Can we talk for a moment?" he asked softly.

Mary nodded, though she would have preferred to be alone.

Reverend McDee sat down, though not without some effort. His muscles had become used to chairs.

"Rough days," he stated flatly.

Mary nodded. "Yes," she said softly.

"Death is never an easy issue, Mary. That's especially true when it's a child. Tell me, do you believe your child's soul is in heaven?"

"I do, Reverend," answered Mary. "But I think I believe it out of desperation more than conviction."

McDee nodded. "Your hope is justified in the book of Deuteronomy it says, and I think I can recall exactly, '...and sons and daughters, who this day have no knowledge of good or evil, shall enter heaven, and I will give it to them and they shall possess it.' Also, in Job where it talks about miscarriages, it says they shall rest with Him."

"As Christians, we believe the Bible contains the Holy Word of God and we live our lives dedicated to that Word and the lifestyle it commands, don't we?"

Mary nodded silently.

"It is our confidence in God's Word that allows us to survive the tragedies of this life."

"That's so much easier said than done, isn't it?" asked Mary.

"Yes, I agree, Mary. Still, despite how hard it is at times, we cling to our faith in the most desperate times. And this is certainly one of your most desperate times. So, my counsel is this: If Jesus was given a soul before birth, as the Bible indicates, then He gave us one too. Because Jesus was born as a human, lived as a human, died as a human, and was brought into heaven with His divine soul, we should expect no less."

"Your baby, Mary, I believe is now singing the songs of angels. Even if earthly life ended before a first breath, her eternal soul lives on. As her soul was alive before being placed within your daughter, it now lives as a new creature in God's kingdom. The souls of the unborn shall rejoice, as we all shall when united in our heavenly home, as promised so long ago."

"So, you believe she is in heaven?" asked Mary, her voice barely audible.

"I do."

"You believe her soul was alive long before it was placed within her tiny body?"

McDee nodded, "Yes, I do. Your baby has an old soul, as do we all."

Mary nodded slowly, taking a deep breath. "I believe that, too."

"Yes, our tears during these times are for ourselves. It is our sorrow which we bear for the loss we suffer. Cry your tears, Mary, heal your heart, but keep in mind that your daughter sings with angels."

"But why? I don't understand why. She didn't get to accept or reject Christ. She didn't get a chance at anything. What possible purpose could her death have?"

Reverend McDee slowly rose from the ground with a groan. "I gotta stop this business of getting up and down," he mumbled. Then wiping his hands on his pants was silent while gathering his thoughts.

"I wish I had a pat answer to that; one which would bring comfort to you, but I don't. It's above my pay grade." McDee took a deep breath before continuing. "However, I have a personal opinion. I don't share it often because I may be wrong and I don't want to mislead anyone. But here it is: I believe the Earth was created so the souls alive in heaven could become new creatures here on Earth and in the hereafter."

"New creatures?"

McDee nodded. "I believe Satan has contaminated heaven with his evil. This contamination occurred millenniums ago. Heaven is no longer a place which is holy and where God can live among his people, for God cannot tolerate evil. While originally a holy place, Lucifer brought sin into it. Because of this sin, God needed to create a new heavenly home based upon something that was incorruptible. He did, it's called – faith. Everything in our heavenly home was now contaminated by sin. So, God needed to create a new home for us to inhabit, and create a new relationship between us, uncontaminated by the manipulation of His Holy Word. He created Earth so our souls in heaven could establish a new relationship with him in a new Earth. That relationship is faith. God placed our souls within these bodies, providing a home for faith, for Him. No longer is our relationship only the written Word. We must live by faith. We shall become new creatures of faith ready to share with our creator in the future a New Heaven and New Earth promised in the Bible – holy and uncontaminated by the evils of Satan."

"But our daughter never lived."

"But, I believe she did. When she was created she was blessed with a soul that lived long before this age and that soul continues to live today. She is now a new creature of God as you and I shall be in the hereafter."

"So, you believe she lives."

"I do. I believe her soul lives today. And someday she shall sing with you in the New Heaven."

Mary was silent.

"Well, I'll leave you to your thoughts, Mary," said McDee.

Mary silently nodded.

* * * * *

In the days that followed, winter gradually turned to spring, even though the normal warming rays of the sun were diminished by the airborne debris from the volcanoes, which reduced the spring temperatures everywhere. Roy and Betty said they had never, in their lives, seen so many days of bone-chilling spring temperatures.

Though the temperatures some nights dropped to near zero, other days were seventy degrees when the grey-black skies turned blue. The cable on the television was out, but Roy found some rabbit-ear antennas in the barn. With some adjustment they were able, at times, to tune in the station near Asheville where they got some good news. The debris from the Volcanoes was clearing and it was expected the summer temperatures would soon be close to normal.

That forecast proved only partially correct. The ash did clear somewhat, but only allowed the temperatures to occasionally reach above sixty-five. Despite the cool temperatures, Roy insisted on cultivating the garden. So, calling the group together, he approached them about the crops.

"Judging from the change in weather, we obviously are not going to have a normal summer. That means we have to adjust the crops I would normally put in here. There are a number of cool weather crops we could grow. I think the most practical would include: lettuce, peas, carrots, broccoli and cauliflower."

"What's Broklli?" asked Alison.

"What's Kalifowers?" chimed Katie.

"They are delicious veggies and I hear they make little girls beautiful," replied Margie Stewart.

"That's why I don't eat them," smiled Tim. "I don't wanna be any more pretty than I am."

Roy continued, "I think we ought to consider another crop. I think the foliage around the field has grown high enough we consider putting in some corn. It won't be the best because the growing season is going to be so short, but I sure would like some corn," he smiled.

"Count me in," said Reverend McDee.

"Tell you what I miss, that's roasting the corn on the cob and then eating it," chimed in Betty.

"What about you Mary? Are you in with the corn?"

Mary was quiet for a moment, and then smiled quietly, "Sure."

"Okay, then," said Donny, "It's settled, we'll put in some corn, lettuce, carrots, and peas.

"Don't forget the Broklli!" chimed in Alison

"Or the Kalifowers," said Katie

Smiling, the group dispersed, leaving the details to Donny Stewart and the men volunteering to plant.

Tim started to leave with them, and then turned to Mary who was studying her coffee.

"You aren't looking happy, Honey." He said

Mary looked up and silently looked into her husband's eyes. Finally, smiling said, "I'm fine."

"No, you're not. And I'm sure I know why. You don't think we will ever be able to plant that crop. You don't think we will even be here, do you? It has to do with what you said a while back isn't it? They are coming for us before we even have time to plant one seed."

Mary nodded.

Chapter 12: The Refuge

Jail cells in the Army Stockade were located in the basement of the motor pool. There were only two cells, and both were empty. When the Fort was originally designed, it was not thought to need many cells, considering it was originally half the current size. The prisoners normally there might only be jailed for a short thirty-day sentence, or were transferred to more permanent cells in other locations. Part-time clerk and jailer, Sergeant Scott Jabalee, opened the first cell and the escorting soldiers put the Hermit inside. They were respectful of his advanced age and did not force him in any way. Watching the jailer lock the cell, they were satisfied that their duty was done and left.

"So," said Jabalee, after the soldiers left, "Mr. Kermit, are you comfortable?"

"Oh, yes, young man I'm always comfortable," he smiled.

"Well, if you need anything, let me know. Course, I can't call you a cab," he laughed.

"May I ask a question?" said the Hermit.

"Sure."

"You don't consider yourself a Christian anymore?"

Jabalee looked hard at the old man. "What kind of question is that? How dare you ask a question like that! You know I should report that – they probably will beat you before they shoot you."

The Hermit nodded, "I heard they do things like that. On the other hand, I recall you as a gentle soul. I believe you were once a good Christian. In fact, didn't you play the role of a sheppard in your church's Christmas play?"

Jabalee stared with his mouth half open. "How did you know that, old man?" he asked in a whispered hiss.

"And, if I'm not mistaken, which I am not, didn't you accept membership in St. John Lutheran Church?"

78

Jabalee's anger turned to amazement. "How did you know that? I don't care who you tell, I will deny that! Nobody's gonna believe an old wrinkled nobody like you anyway!"

The Hermit was silent for a moment. "What if I told you an angel whispered that to me?"

"You're a crazy old man – yep, crazy," said Jabalee as he turned to the door. Laying his hand on the handle he turned back, "Nobody would believe you old man, nobody!" he snapped as he slammed the door shut behind him and locked it. Jabalee put the keys on his well-worn wooden desk showing it had served far beyond expectation. Reaching down, Jabalee retrieved his bag of leftovers from lunch. Straightening up, he jumped. "What the–"

Standing in front of his desk was the Hermit.

"Well, Mr. Jabalee, I enjoyed my stay, but I must go now," he said.

"How did you–"

"People are asking things like that all the time. The important thing is for you to leave. Once they find out I am gone, you will be arrested and shot. Shot for sure when they look into your background and find you went to St John Lutheran Church. I assure you they will find that out when they investigate you after I escape – I believe that's what they will call it – an escape."

Jabalee was unable to speak.

"I came here because soon others will be brought here. Christians, just like you used to consider yourself. I suggest you consider letting them go, and going with them. They are your only hope now."

"What are you talking about!" shouted Jabalee. "I'm not going anywhere, and you aren't either! Get back in your cell, or I'll shoot you!"

As quickly as his rotund body would allow, Jabalee reached for the firearm in the holster, but the safety strap prevented a quick draw. Finally withdrawing it, he pointed at the Hermit. "Do you hear me?"

"Of course I do, Scott. Now, you listen to me. It's time for you to come back to Jesus. The people that are being brought will help you do that."

"I'm only gonna say it one more time, then I'm pulling the trigger – and I ain't kidding!" warned Jabalee, as he raised the pistol so that it pointed straight at the Hermit's chest. "Get back into..." His voice trailed off as the image of his prisoner faded into nothing.

For a second, Jabalee was about to scream, then covered his mouth with his left hand. Laying his gun on the desk he sat down in his chair, stunned.

* * * * *

It was a quiet day as Mary and Margie prepared a sparse lunch. The others were either taking naps or thinking about it.

"Well darlin'," began Margie, "when do you think we should be goin' to that other place you was talking about?"

"The cave?"

"Yes."

"Not yet, Margie – but soon."

"Well, I was thinking we should pack some of our clothes and stuff. Will you give us enough time to do that?"

"We won't be taking anything, I'm afraid."

From outside Roy opened the screen door in a panic. "Company!" he shouted as he rushed to retrieve his rifle.

"No, Roy!" shouted Mary. "Leave the guns alone. Everyone leave the guns alone!"

All rushed the windows to see who was coming down the drive. There were three vehicles, one half-ton truck, a Humvee, followed by a long Transit school bus painted with army colors and insignia. It looked capable of seating eighty passengers.

"It's the army!" shouted Donny. "Margie!" he shouted.

"Here, Grandpa," she answered,

"Get below – remember to be quiet."

Mary threw up her arms and shouted for silence. "I told you about this. Remain calm and don't panic. God knows about this. All will be well if we just trust Him."

The group became quiet.

"Roy, don't have Margie go down, keep her with you – all will be well in the end."

Outside, the vehicles faced the farm-house for a moment in silence. Then, from the rear of the one with the canvas covered truck, soldiers dismounted and approached the house with their weapons at the ready. An officer raised a bullhorn.

"You, inside the house, come out with your hands in the air!"

For a few minutes all remained silent, then from the side door, Mary came out with the others following her. They all had their hands straight up or on the top of their heads. The twins mimicked the others and came with raised hands.

"Which one of you is Brunswick?" shouted Bellmore

Brunswick smiled and came forward. Captain Bellmore returned the smile offering his hand, "Good work Sergeant."

"Thank you, sir."

"So, is this all of them?"

"Yes, sir, at least here. There's another camp called Camp New Adam. I've tried to get the location, but haven't had any luck."

"What have you learned about this other camp?"

"Not much; however, there are two men, McDee and Harkins, who visited it and know its location and all the details. When you start your interrogation, I suggest you start with them."

Bellmore nodded with a grunt. Then turning to his men commanded, "Okay, put them in restraints and pack 'em up!" Several soldiers came forward putting the arms of their captives behind their backs and attaching the standard Monadn plastic cuffs. With only the minimal amount of communication, the group was led individually to the brown army bus. The only sound came as the twins were brought to the bus where they began to cry. Once inside the vehicle, the twins snuggled up to Mary, while Margie clung to Nora, but it didn't stop their tears.

When the group was loaded onto the bus, two armed guards sat in the seats immediately behind the driver. The prisoners were told to sit in the rear of the long bus.

It was almost a two-hour ride to the fort, and the children eventually fell asleep. There was no communication at all between the adults, and drew sharp rebukes from the guards the two times it was attempted.

Finally reaching the arch spanning the entrance to Fort Smith, Tim noticed how sterile the camp appeared. Although there were a few soldiers walking about, the camp appeared almost deserted, though absolutely clean and orderly. Passing through the outer circular drive they entered an inner circular area. Buildings lined this inner circle on the outside, while within the circle there was a place for cars to park around an inner round area of grass. The bus turned down a narrow side street where he backed between two old buildings, stopping next to a cement stairway leading down to a basement.

Instructed to exit the bus, the Christians were escorted down cement stairs to the lower level. Here they entered a room with several desks, only one of which was occupied.

"We got visitors for you," said Captain Bellmore.

Sergeant Jabalee at the desk stood up, but appeared unsure of himself.

Bellmore motioned the guards forward with the prisoners.

Grabbing the keys on the desk, Jabalee opened the door to the cell.

"A little crowded with just two cells, don't you think?" asked Tim.

"Shut up!" snapped Bellmore.

Silently the group went inside with only the sniffling twins breaking the silence.

Bellmore turned to Jabalee with a finger shaking in his face. "I don't want anyone visiting them, do you understand me?"

"Yes, sir, no visitors."

Bellmore gave one last glance to the prisoners before walking out and continuing out the main entrance. With a lingering look, Jabalee smiled briefly and locked the outer door.

Left alone in the cells, the men remained standing while the women and children sat on the two wooden benches.

"So, this is God at work?" mumbled Tim in close to a sarcastic tone.

"Maybe," said Reverend McDee in a slow voice.

"So now what?" asked Donny.

"Now we wait," replied Mary. "Let's give God a chance. I think we have to stop pre-judging Him. Maybe this is where we shall die, maybe not. If it is, then let's keep in mind that the purpose of our soul's life is not to just live. We are on a journey, and this is just one stop."

"Well, honey, I don't mean to be a downer, but I sorta don't like this stop," said Tim.

They heard the key turning in the outer door and Jabalee walked in. For a moment he hesitated.

"Do you folks know an old guy named Kermit?"

The two twins squealed, "Yes, we know him!"

Mary followed up by smiling, "Yes, we know him. His name is actually The Hermit – at least that's how we've come to know him over time."

Jabalee came forward. "That guy is really spooky. Is he some kind of angel or something?"

Reverend McDee smiled, "That's what I think he is, and I think most people who get to know him will say the same." Briefly Jabalee recounted his experience with the Hermit, concluding, "...then he just up and faded away. Now, I know it sounds nuts, but I swear the old guy just faded away into nothing! I don't mind tellin' you, it scared me to death."

Mary smiled, "Oh, no need for that. The Hermit is a friend to the faithful."

"Well, that brings me to what I need to talk to you about. He was right, used to be I was a Christian. I grew up at St John Lutheran Church, and when I was seventeen, I accepted Jesus as my Savior and became a member of the church. It was a happy day for me – and for my parents, God rest their souls."

"And now?"

"Well," began Jabalee. "Over the years, I guess I just drifted away. And then these Space Guys showed up and talking how Christians and Jews were just into fantasy – well, I guess I just bought it."

"And now?" asked McDee.

"It's been bothering me lately. Course I never told anybody, and then this old guy shows up and nails me. I mean he knew me from the inside out." Jabalee paused, looked at the floor and shuffled his feet. "The old guy sorta suggested that I go with you folks."

"Go with us?" asked Tim.

Jabalee nodded. "Of course, I would let you guys out and then go with you."

"Let me ask you this," said Mary. "Do you want to give yourself over to Christ again?"

Jabalee walked a few steps forward so that he was facing Mary. "Yes, I never knew how much I missed Him 'til that Kermit or Hermit started talking."

"You can start by letting us out of this cell," ventured Tim.

Quickly Jabalee produced the keys and unlocked the cell. Immediately Tim and Harkins went to the outer office with the others following. Only Mary stayed behind with Jabalee.

"Give me your hand," she said quietly.

Jabalee presented his right hand with the Mark clearly upon it.

Mary took his hand between her own and closed her eyes. "I'm sensing your soul is indeed a child of Jesus," she smiled. Then she had Jabalee reaffirm his love of Christ and His role as Savior. When he concluded she released his hand.

Jabalee let out a shout as he saw the Mark was no longer on his hand, and immediately kneeled to Mary. "Thank You. I don't care if they want to kill me, I will never again deny who I am. Thank you, Holy Mary!"

"Stop that!" snapped Mary. "I'm no different than you or anybody else. I've simply had a longer relationship with the Lord. You will do similar things in time. Now grow your faith, allowing Christ to teach you how."

Jabalee stood up. "Yes, I will – and thank you, thank you again."

Mary hurried to the outer office where the others, except for Sergeant Harkins were waiting. She was about to ask where he was when they heard him open the outer door and come down the steps.

"Outside is the bus that brought us here, they haven't moved it – and the keys are still in the ignition!"

"Praise God!" shouted Betty with others echoing her.

Mary turned to Jabalee with a questioning look.

"I'm not going, Mary," he said. "I've changed my mind."

"Not going with us?"

"No, I need to stay here. I know others who are now hiding their relationship with God, as I did. I don't know if I can help them regain it or not, but I must try. I have to make up for all the time I denied Him."

Mary hugged him. "I understand, I really do," she said.

"Let's go!" shouted Tim. At the outer door, Tim opened the door and looked out. Seeing no one, he ran to the bus with others following.

"I'll drive!" shouted Harkins entering the bus. Immediately he started the bus and checked the instruments he was familiar with from training. Waiting for Donny Stewart, the last person

85

to enter, he shut the door, put the bus in reverse, and slowly backed out on to the road. There was no traffic, nor any sign of anyone.

Slowly, he drove the bus out of the Fort exchanging a wave with the unsuspecting Gate Guard.

"Where are you headed?" asked Mary

"I have no idea, I just wanted to get outta that place." smiled Harkins.

"We need to get back to the farm!" shouted Margie.

"We can't," responded Roy. "They know that's where we came from, and probably where we'll return."

Mary stood up and faced the others, keeping her balance by holding onto the seat. "I think we should go where Reverend McDee and Sergeant Harkins found those Christians. The way there will take us past your farm."

"Yes, definitely," chimed McDee.

"What's the point of what we just went through?" asked Tim. "We were going there to begin with, now we're headed again. What was the whole point of being arrested if we just are going there again?"

"Oh stop it Tim!" hissed Mary. "Stop taking every opportunity you can to badmouth God. Who do you think you are? Does God have to justify everything He does to you? Sometimes we see His reasons, sometimes we don't. We aren't on a journey to justify God; we're on a journey to gain faith!"

"Well, if you ask me," injected Harkins, "That jail guard is one reason – maybe one soul is just that important." Tim looked at Mary for a moment, shook his head and went to the back of the bus.

"Now, when we pass by the farm," offered Donny, "maybe we could stop just for a bit."

Mary considered for a moment. "We'll see, but I don't have a good feeling about it."

Harkins drove, careful not to exceed the limit. Donny and Tim in the rear of the bus kept an eye out for anyone following them. Outrunning even the slowest pursuer was out of the question for the bus.

Finally, they turned down the road which ran past their farm.

"I don't feel good about stopping, Margie," said Mary, then to Harkins, "Scott, when we reach the farm don't stop, keep going."

Chapter 13: The Pyramid

Valice found himself squirming in his seat. Even getting up occasionally to walk the aisle was only partially successful in quieting his muscles. The fatigue of the final four-hour leg of their flight was seeping into his bones. Though the plane's interior had been custom designed for senior officers, it failed to ease his growing discomfort. As with all such planes for Colonels and above, the seats were custom with some facing each other and a coffee table between. It resembled more a doctor's waiting room than an Air Force aircraft. Such was the life of senior officers.

Of the fourteen districts, seven District Commissioners were aboard the aircraft including Valice. There were two colonels, one brigadier general, a major general, and one four-star general. It was quickly determined that no one knew the purpose of being assembled. The ash was light enough to allow this and other aircraft to fly to the pyramid. Normally, only ship traffic was being permitted.

Only a few of those on the plane had met each other during their careers. There was speculation among them why the meeting was called, including one wild guess they were all going to be executed because they'd lost track of so many Christians and Jews. That was quickly dismissed, as much out of hope as conviction.

From there, they drifted into small talk and good-natured joking; however, all fell into the hole of private thoughts the nearer they got to the pyramid.

Valice hadn't mingled too much with the others, other than the extent required by manners. All were Commanding Commissioners over one of the Districts in the U.S. Valice commanded Ohio, Kentucky and West Virginia. Soon he, as temporary command of District Five, would add Tennessee, South Carolina, and North Carolina. It was a command more fitting of his rank. The combined states would bring his command to over thirty-nine million citizens. Only Districts Ten and Fourteen would have as many. The thought of it brought a smile to his face. He wondered if any of those on the plane knew, and he wondered about their reactions when they found out. Again, he smiled.

As the plane neared the pyramid, it banked to the left giving those on his side of the aircraft their first live view of the it. There were a few gasps at the sheer size of the structure which assaulted their senses. It looked more like an island than something that had been constructed. The plane was at two thousand feet in its descent and the spire of the pyramid far above them, disappearing into the light cloud cover.

The northern edge was not visible at the base of the pyramid and the metal skirt surrounding it was miles in length, fading from view in the combined salt air, slight ash and morning mist. Valice had read about the size of this final and largest pyramid – it seemed impossible such a thing could even make it into space. It was said there was no visual recording or witness to its plunge from orbit around Earth to the sea because it occurred at night, out of sight of land or ship – a fact the television networks bemoaned, having missed one of the truly monumental sights of the modern world.

Their plane circled then leveled for the final approach. When it touched down on the metal runway, the outer seaside of the metal skirt was out of sight. Rising above them, into the clouds, was the silver pyramid. The plane taxied down yellow stripes painted on the metal to a spot approximately a quarter mile to the main entrance. Transportation was waiting for them. It was some type of vehicle that, Valice guessed, would accommodate near a hundred people. It silently floated approximately six inches off the deck and was unmanned. The doors, one located in the front and the other towards the rear, closed silently when they all had entered, then it quietly made its way to the main entrance of the pyramid. The opening was less than three to four hundred feet wide, if not more. Through it passed hundreds of people, some going out and some in. Added to the people were transports like the one that held them. It felt odd to Valice that there was very little conversation between the seven of them. It confirmed that all, including himself, were worried about this meeting. Slowly the transport weaved its way through the huge lobby and down one of the many corridor avenues which radiated off the entrance. Finally, after a breathtaking ride on an elevator, the transport began letting the officers out, flashing each name from a display overhead when it stopped. From a slot directly under the screen, a plastic card appeared, and the screen directed him to take it. Valice was the fourth stop at his room numbered 7523819. He took his own bag from transport and slipped his card into the door as the transporter whined away.

Inside the quarters which were obviously designated for senior officers, he found very comfortable accommodations. This didn't surprise him as he had visited the old pyramids where the apartments were the same. Throwing his bag on the bed in the bedroom, he ventured to the living room and the floor-to-ceiling window where he could see the activities below. The buzzing of the room communications startled him. Answering it he smiled at the voice of Colonel Alan Tux, District Commissioner of Area Nine. Tony found Alan's personality suited his own.

"Tony," said Colonel Tux, "Ready for some company?"

"Sure Al, come on over. Where is your room?"

"Actually, I'm only two rooms away. I'll be right there."

True to his word, a knock followed a few minutes later. Tony let him in and after some good-natured humor escorted him into the living room.

As Tux sat down his mood changed. He looked at Valice with a solemn face. "Why are we here, Tony?"

"I haven't got a clue – I know as far as I'm concerned, I'm supposed to meet with the Prefect 'cause they've given me

District 5 in addition to my own, at least temporarily. I'm hoping they make it permanent and combine them."

Tux whistled. "Now that's some news! Congratulations, that brings you past the magic thirty-mill mark."

"Actually, thirty-nine million."

"I thought you were too senior to have only the eighteen-mill of District 4." Tux paused. "But why do you think they want both of us here?"

"Well, I've given it some thought, and I think it has to do with all those Christians escaping."

Tux nodded thoughtfully. "Yeah, I'm sure you're right. What do you think happened?"

"I have no idea – you know what some folks are saying?"

"Yeah, I hear them using the word Rapture, but I stifle that crap." Then added, "Let's hope it's not that," he laughed. Valice smiled in return. "No, I think somehow these folks had a communication network set up, and it was a coordinated action."

Tux was silent as he rubbed his face with his hands, as if encouraging his mind to work. "Between you and I, do you think that Rapture thing is possible?"

Valice was silent. He liked Tux and trusted him; however, in times like these, one had to be careful what was said. The adage 'loose lips sink ships' came to his mind. "Oh, I think there's no reason for us to stretch our minds on this. We'll find out soon enough at the meeting. So, how 'bout a drink?"

Tux smiled, "I knew there was a reason to visit an ugly buzzard like you!"

The two men spent the rest of the evening exchanging war stories and family news. It was well into the night before they parted.

The next morning Valice was up early, despite the late night. The scheduled meeting was in less than two hours and although he felt a small twinge of anxiousness, he hoped it wouldn't mature into fear. Quickly shaving and dressing, he

91

made his way to the Officers' Mess Hall. The trip down the elevator left his stomach far behind as it plunged. The elevators were, thus far, his most distasteful experience aboard any of the pyramids.

At breakfast in the senior officers' section he ordered his favorite: eggs, bacon, biscuits, and gravy, along with toast and coffee. On the pyramids, one could still get three decent meals a day, unlike on land where most of the restaurants were closed, and the ones still open would not make any best-restaurant list. He saw two other District Commissioners: Lt. General Gilbert and Colonel Lutfy, but he did not say hello to them nor they to him.

Valice lingered over his coffee until he felt it was time to go the meeting. In the large hallway, transports were waiting. Valice got in one. His voice command of the room number was all that was needed to start the vehicle on its way. A couple minutes later the door opened, and he entered the designated meeting room where he found two junior army soldiers occupying desks at opposite ends of the room.

Valice approached the first and then was directed to the second. He was asked to have a seat, but did not have to wait long before an army corporal came for him and took him to the meeting room. Entering the room, he saw a large circular desk the appropriate number of seats, of which several were already occupied.

He nodded to Tux and a couple others, but no conversation was offered. Finding his name place, Valice took his seat. One by one, the other District Commissioners came into the nearly silent room and took their seats. All sat quietly for ten minutes when three black robbed figures entered from the side door. They walked to a podium facing the waiting group.

"Good morning gentlemen," said the figure in the middle. Valice recognized him as Durk, the alien who had said he was getting District 5. His voice was very low and had resonance to it.

The assembled officers gave muffled returned greetings, neither loud nor enthusiastic.

Durk nodded. "Do you know why you have been called here?"

It was Colonel Lutfy who volunteered an answer. "The disappearance of the Christians, I think," he said.

Valice almost started to shake his head, but stopped. Lutfy would never make his first star if he kept volunteering stuff like this.

For a moment Durk studied Lutfy. "Colonel Lutfy you are correct. That and other things I know are on your minds. Tell me, Colonel Lutfy, where do you think the Christians are?"

Lutfy was taken aback by the question; he licked his lips to buy time. Finally, straightening up a bit, he ventured, "I don't know. There is talk that the Jesus Freaks had their Rapture."

"Don't use that word!" shouted Durk with a volume that made some of the generals put their hands over their ears, while a couple others held up hands in front of the faces as if that could stop the deafening sound. Durk seemed to recover his composure and looked at Lutfy. "Where did you hear that abominable word?"

Lutfy was clearly shaken. "Well, ah, I heard some of the Christian prisoners use it."

Durk was silent for a moment. Then, regaining his composure continued. "This is just Christian trash talk. Even the thought of such a thing is absolutely ridiculous and an affront to all we stand for here." The last was followed by a smile, which brought some nervous laughter from some.

"This is so illogical – it is an affront to our minds, and I do not want to hear that word ever again. How can you lead your fellow citizens to their homes in the stars when you continue to spout such illogical and demeaning remarks?" No one answered but a few nodded their agreement.

"Now, I know many of these fanatics perished in the natural disasters which visited the earth – as did many of our own group. But I repeat these were natural disasters – in fact, we told you such things were coming!" Durk walked a couple paces to his left while in thought. "So, the first reason I brought you here was to make sure you knew these were predicted disasters and nothing more. However, there is a second reason which is more serious than this." Again, he looked at each Commissioner before resuming. "Have you heard anything about the Mark being worn by Christians?" Each of the Commissioners again cast looks at one another and shook their heads.

Durk nodded before speaking, "I'm sad to say, it's true. In fact, we believe that's where all the Christians went. They are now wearing the Mark to hide from us. This deception is the main reason you've been called here."

"I don't understand. Are you saying there are Christians running around with the Mark? How can that be?" asked Brigadier General Damon of District 1.

"It does not matter how it can be, there are instances where it has happened – and it seems to be increasing."

"I thought such a thing was impossible."

Durk smiled, "Apparently life is more important to them than their phony religion."

"How are we supposed to tell the difference between those who are clean and those who have the religious filth?" asked General Damon.

"Yes, exactly," replied Durk. "You cannot. So, we must have a new two-point program. First: we need to change our methods of identifying Christians. Second: those of us who are your Ancestral Brothers need to bring some of our expertise to your aid. We know what must be done and will help those who are hesitant." Durk looked around at the expectant faces. "The first part involves a great scrutiny of the populations you govern. Up 'til now, the Mark itself was our guide; however, now we have to look at behavior. First, those who received the Mark initially seem to be more loyal; while those who have received the Mark within the last year or so, are the fertile grounds for traitors."

"Are there types of behavior that we can identify?" asked Tucker.

"Other than the obvious, there aren't any; so, you and those under your command will have to use their own judgment."

"I don't understand," said Lutfy. "Are you saying they just see someone and make a decision based on how they walk or talk as to whether he is a Christian?"

Durk nodded slowly. "Initially we thought challenging people to curse the name of their so-called savior – and please don't mention that filthy name here – would work. We thought these so-called Christians would refuse to do that. However, our experience is that this is not the case. Besides, it takes too long. I know, it is a terrible responsibility we are giving to the common soldier, but the time grows short. The disasters you have just witnessed are only preliminary. Those to come are many times as great and will kill many, many more – including many of those who would go to the stars with you. Even your lives are at stake and those of your families, because who knows where the next disaster will strike?"

General Damon cleared his throat, as he usually did before speaking. "I don't believe our troops will execute people based on a hunch, even though they have dedicated themselves to the Brothers."

Durk nodded. "I believe you are right, therefore I think we need to enlist the help of those who you call Goonies. First, I will increase the reward for evidence they have eliminated someone sympathetic to the Fanatics. You need to let them know you support their efforts, and you will lend assistance if they uncover a group of the Fanatics."

"Lastly, we are going to give you some help. We will be assigning one of our own to the headquarters of each of the Districts around the globe. They will assist you in carrying out this campaign to save the lives of those dedicated to leaving this doomed planet, including your own loved ones."

This announcement was greeted with a silence that hung over the group.

"A word to the wise, gentlemen," said Durk in a lowered tone. "Our representative will be watching your population, but will also be watching you. I hope you will not give him reason to doubt your own loyalty."

"I can assure you, sir," responded Damon, "We are all loyal to the cause."

Chapter 14: Valice

As they neared their home Margie gasped. The house was now only a collection of charred and burnt remains. The building in the rear was not much better. Though the sides still stood, there was no roof and the marks on the front indicated the fire had completely destroyed the interior. There was no sign of the chickens.

Harkins slowed as the Stewarts looked at their beloved home, now devastated by wandering Goonies. Donny put his arm around his wife as Margie shed tears and Donny was close to joining her.

McDee stepped forward as Harkins stopped the bus. "I don't want to make less of your grief, but I think God rescued us from this when he had us arrested."

There was a murmur of agreement.

"Yes, we're lucky we weren't here when this happened," said Harkins. "Can you imagine what would have happened if a troop of Goonies came?"

Donny nodded slowly. "I think you're right. God hid us from the Goonies inside a prison cell."

"Do you want to go in?" asked Harkins.

Donny shook his head. "No, I don't think we want to see any more."

Harkins slowly accelerated. About a mile down the road they saw the house of their neighbors also burnt to the ground

"Let's just check to see if the ladies survived," said Mary.

Harkins slowed then turned into the gravel drive. The house had been a two-story structure, half of which remained, while the other was a charred assortment of lumber resting on a cement slab.

"Why don't you folks wait here?" suggested Roy as he grabbed his gun. "Harkins and I will take a look around. If they're alive they might recognize me and not run."

Opening the bus doors, Harkins ventured out with Roy behind. There was no indication of life either human or animal. Slowly they approached the house, but seeing no evidence of the occupants, went to the barn. While showing some fire damage, the barn was still mostly intact.

Roy took up a position at the open door to cover Harkins as he entered the building.

Harkins motioned for Roy to angle to his right while Harkins went left. There were no animals visible in the barn, though there were signs and smells indicating that some had been there recently.

Suddenly, Harkins stopped. "Here, Roy – come here."

Roy made his way over to Harkins, still keeping an eye on the barn floor.

"Oh, no," he said arriving. Lying in the third stall were the bodies of the farm's elderly owners. Both ladies were missing their right hands.

Venturing further into the barn didn't yield any sign of life, and both men backed out. "We found the bodies of the owners," said Harkins as he returned to the bus. "They were both handed."

"Oh, no!" said Betty covering her face.

"I think it's time we set out a plan for ourselves," McDee said.

Roy turned, "I think we should just start driving northwest toward Michigan. I hear there might be some areas in the Great Lakes, near the Canadian border, that aren't quite under the Brother's total control. Maybe we can find one."

"I don't see how we can," replied Tim. "How are we going to get the gas to get that far, plus with a bus, we are sure to be stopped sooner or later."

"We could siphon the gas – I use to do that as a kid, you know," smiled Roy. "Plus, if we stick to the country roads we just make it through."

Mary stood up. "I think the best thing for us to do is go to that place Roy and Sergeant Harkins found – what did they call it, Scott?"

"Camp New Adam," replied Harkins.

"And did you get the impression they would welcome us?"

"I think they would, they are especially anxious to have people without the Mark join them. I think they believe it would give them some sorta legitimacy with God, or something," said Harkins.

Betty spoke up. "You say they all have the Mark; how do you know if they aren't just trying to lure us there for the reward?"

"Well, Betty, Roy had the Mark, but he is obviously a Christian," said Mary.

Betty nodded silently.

"I assume you and Roy could lead us back to the tunnel?" asked Mary.

Harkins nodded. "Absolutely; it wouldn't be hard."

Mary smiled, "Well then, Sergeant, why don't you get us going?"

* * * * *

The return trip to his headquarters was too short. Brigadier General Tony Valice would have preferred a trip twice as long. His mind was filled with mixed emotions after his visit to the Pyramid. He'd considered himself a dedicated soldier who protected his country and its citizens for over twenty years. Valice was proud of his service, and his family was proud of him. He'd saluted the flag so many times over those years, he probably built some arm muscles. Wherever he was, when he heard the National Anthem being played he'd come to attention and salute, or place his hand over his heart.

Now he dreaded going through those gates, dreaded going up the stairs, entering the office and taking his seat of command. For the first time in his life, he was ashamed of being a soldier.

To his regret, his trip ended with the plane landing. A quick ride to the other side of the airport brought him to the chopper followed by a too-short forty-five minute flight to the Fort. He always loved taking the chopper. It soared at a height where he could maintain contact with the farms, houses, towns – even with the animals that scattered hearing the beat of the blade barely a couple hundred feet or so above. But today there was no joy.

The miles from Asheville to Fort Smith seemed to pass too quickly. As they drew closer, the feeling of dread grew. The chopper landed on the pad in the inner circle of the parking area. Quickly thanking the crew, Valice walked to the building housing his office.

Entering the outer office, he nodded greetings to the staff as he made his way to his desk while motioning Capt. Bellmore and Sergeant Sterling to follow.

General Valice sat down at his desk and signaled for the Sergeant to close the door.

"Did you have a good trip?" asked Captain Bellmore, hoping to set a relaxed tone to the discussion.

Ignoring the remark, he looked at Bellmore. "Tell me, Danny, how did things go here?"

Bellmore's body language would have told even an uneducated man that the Captain was unnerved by the question, though he knew it would be asked. "Well sir, I've got some bad news on that front. I believe you got our message that we'd captured a Christian."

"Um, yes, some old man."

"Well, yes. I instructed Sergeant Sterling to put him in jail."

"Which I did," interrupted Sterling. "And I saw the jailer lock the cell door – and the outer door..."

"...but, now he's gone," injected Bellmore.

"Escaped, eh?" asked Valice with a disinterested tone.

"Yes, sir," said Captain Bellmore, with a quick glance at Sergeant Sterling. "We wanted to ask the guard what happened, but we can't find him."

"Missing? Okay; I'm sure that he will show up again, how far can he run? Is that all?" asked Valice.

"Well, one more thing," began Bellmore, nerves showing in his voice. "We captured nine Christians not far from where we picked up that old man. We brought them in and were holding them for you."

"Yes, so I heard. Well, good," responded Valice in a monotone.

"Ah, that's where this gets weird. They escaped, too."

For the first time Valice showed some interest. "Now let me get this straight. You locked up the old man, and he escaped. You locked up more Christians and they escaped, too? And the guard is missing? Is that right?"

Both Valice and Sterling nodded without uttering a sound.

General Valice looked sternly at first one and then the other. For several seconds there was absolute silence in the room. The first indication that there was a reaction was a small smile that began playing with the lips of Valice, it eventually grew and ended with Valice first chuckling and then bursting out in laughter and slapping his desk. Finally, he found his voice and ordered, "Get out!" between his guffaws.

Glancing at each other the two quickly left closing the door behind them.

Valice continued to laugh slowly, only his rocking shoulders showing his mirth; however, while the shoulders continued to shake, the eyes began birthing tears. Finally, Valice covered his face and quietly shed the kind of tears he hadn't since boyhood. It'd been so long since he'd actually cried he was surprised he remembered how.

Eventually, he sat up. Wiping his tears away, he took a deep breath, and got up. He took another deep breath, cleared his throat and opened his office door.

Sterling looked up with anticipation, but Valice simply said. "I'm going out."

"Do you need your driver, sir?"

Valice did not reply, but simply waved his hand in denial. Walking down the steps to his staff car where it was parked at the front door. Checking the ignition for keys he got inside. It took only five minutes to drive to the army housing where his home was located.

Entering the house, he saw his wife in the kitchen where he reached out and gently wrapped his arms around her. "I love you, don't you know?"

"Well, of course – and I love you," answered Dora. Her expression showed some bewilderment. This was not like her husband. In addition, she couldn't remember the last time he came home in the middle of the day.

Valice looked into her eyes and smiled, "I'll be in the den," he said in a low voice.

Dora watched him leave. "Is there anything wrong, dear?"

Valice shook his head but did not turn around. Reaching the Den, he went to the window and looked out at the other homes of officers who he commanded. The army had been good to him, and he to it. He fought in two wars, led men to victory, was wounded twice and had always tried his best for his country and men and women under his command.

Slowly he turned and opened the bottom drawer of his desk. Shoving aside some items he finally felt his fingers close on the steel of his forty-five-caliber pistol. Bringing it out, he checked the clip to see that it was full, and that one was in the chamber. Placing the gun on the desk, he took off his uniform jacket. It would be needed later, clean.

The door to the den opened and his wife came in.

"Honey," said Valice, "could you excuse me? I need to be alone right now."

"What's going on? Why are you home? Do you feel alright?" She looked at his desk. "Why is that gun out?"

Valice smiled, but couldn't hold it. "Well Dora darlin' you're right, I don't feel good." He leaned forward, placing his hands on the desk and took a deep breath. he then looked at his wife, who began to shuffle under his gaze. "When I joined this man's army I had high hopes and lots of dreams of the soldier I'd be someday. When I married you, I wanted you to be proud of me..."

"And I have been and still am," interrupted Dora.

"So was I honey, so was I. You know a lot of my efforts were because of you. The fact that you were proud was very important to me. But that is in the past. I'm no longer proud – not now, nor should you be either. Not since these jerks have taken over." Valice ran his hand through his hair. "Oh, at first I was all gung-ho. Here they were taking us to the stars. I dreamed you and I would see and do wonderful things." Valice stood up and smiled. "You know I was never a religious guy. I thought all that was a bunch of hooey people put together to keep other people in line."

"But you've always been a good person, a good man."

"I've tried. But now I see I failed. I'm not a good person. The army I loved has turned me into a murderer of men, women, and children." Valice came to the front of the desk. "You know what they want me to do now?" he asked, but did not wait for an answer. "They want me to just go out and shoot whoever I want and claim it's because they are a religious fanatic. And hear this, they are sending one of those robed jerks to make sure I do it."

"That's awful. How can they do that?"

"Oh, believe me, they can do that."

Valice and Dora were silent for a moment as they looked at each other.

"I always wanted children, did you know that?"

Dora nodded silently.

"We never talked about it. I guess I thought it was just a matter of time. Then, time passed and the more it did the more thought it wouldn't happen. I thought about talking to you, but then I wondered if I should. I didn't want you to feel guilty or maybe it was that I didn't want to feel guilty. Whatever, I just wished we'd had some children."

Dora smiled small as tears found paths down her cheeks. "I know you did." She took a breath before continuing. "I was afraid to talk to you about it, 'cause I thought it was my fault, and worse I thought you thought it was my fault." Dora covered her face with her hands.

Valice stepped forward and wrapped his arms around his wife. For several minutes they stood there rocking back and fell silent in their own thoughts.

Valice looked up at the ceiling as though calling for strength. "There's something else honey, they are sending one of those alien jerks to watch me – checking up, to see I'm killing as many as they think I should."

"What?"

"It's the new directive we received from Prefects and Abdon. Essentially, we are to go out and murder whomever we feel like shooting. The justification is that we think, we suspect, we imagine, we feel they might be, could possibly be, Christian." For a moment silence hung between them. Finally, Valice stroked his wife's hair. "I can't do that Dora. I'm done. But if I refuse to do it, they will accuse me of being a sympathizer and shoot me."

Valice hugged his wife then, continuing to embrace her, slowly walked with her out of the room. There he looked into her eyes.

"I love you, Dora. Please, remember I once was a good man." Giving a slight smile, he walked back into his office.

"What are you going to do?" she said to him.

"It's time I passed sentence upon myself. I'm not going to let those jerks degrade me, put me in front of some firing squad. Dora, I'm responsible for the death of a lot of people, more than you know.

"But, you were just doing what you were told!"

"Oh, others have tried that argument. They hung them just the same, as they should have. No, now it's my time."

"You can't leave me! What will I do without you?"

"Honey, we've been able to save a good sum of money. Use it to go home. When you think of me know even in hell, I'll be thinking about you."

Valice closed the door, and quickly went to the desk and picked up the gun.

As he did, Dora opened the door and screamed "NO!"

Outside their home that afternoon on the quiet street their neighbors heard the single gunshot.

A minute later, there was a second.

Chapter 15: The Mark

"I see it," said McDee, "it's just after that gas station and store. I wonder where the cop car is. Didn't he tell us they stationed themselves there?"

Harkins nodded, "Maybe we'll see him on the gravel road," he said while slowly turning. However, no police car came in sight as they drove the road to the original Camp Adam. At the camp, he made the left turn and headed towards the New Adam. Without warning, a police car shot out blocking their path.

Harkins slammed the brake. Amid frantic grabs for steadying support, there were a few screams.

Donny and Tim reached for their guns on the floor of the bus.

"Hold it!" shouted Mary, "I think this guy might be okay."

"But it's not the cop we saw here before," said Harkins.

"Yeah, still—"

The trooper approached the truck with his hand resting on his sidearm and his eyes glued to the bus and its passengers Without speaking he waved his hand commanding the door be opened.

"Just where are you people headed?"

It was McDee who answered. "We thought we might run into Trooper Thorman."

For a second the trooper remained silent. "How do you know Thorman?"

"He took us to Camp New Adam several months ago," replied McDee. "We were hoping he would remember us."

"Come out slowly and don't make any sudden moves," he commanded stepping back.

Carefully, they each exited the bus as the trooper searched their faces. Finally, Sergeant Harkins brought up the rear.

The trooper studied Harkins as he dismounted.

106

"Wait! I think I do recognize you. You came with another man that Thorman was showing around." A slow smile began to form on his face and he relaxed. "You're the folks without the Mark!"

"Yes, my name is Harkins and I came with this man, Reverend McDee."

"That's me!" smiled McDee waving his hand.

The trooper nodded, "Who are these others?"

"These are the people we told Trooper Thorman about. I know it's been awhile, first the winter, and then the army came and arrested us.

"They let you go?"

"We escaped – it's a long story, but the short of it is they burnt down the farm where we were staying, so we decided to take Trooper Thorman up on his invitation to come here."

The trooper smiled, "Well I'm glad you did. My name is Robert Allen." The trooper said, offering his hand to all. At each, he held their hand for a second examining the smooth backs.

"Okay. You folks follow me," he said after the last handshake.

Returning to his car, the Trooper drove to the fire station with the garage leading to the underground settlement. First instructing Harkins to park the bus, he led the group into the garage where he opened the rear door allowing them access tunnels. After closing the door behind them, they followed down the ramp until reaching level ground. There he turned and indicated they should stop.

"I got some bad news. Dave Thorman is dead."

"Really? What happened?" asked McDee.

"He was shot; actually, executed. I just don't know how they found out. 'Course now they don't need an excuse. At least he didn't tell them anything about this place. Thank God."

"I'm very sorry to hear that," said Harkins. "He seemed like a very good person."

"Are you aware of the new edicts that have gone out?"

The group looked at one another and shook their heads.

"I think that's what happened to Dave. The new deal is they are killing people with and without the Marks."

"What! I thought that was the whole point of the Mark – to allow them to tell the difference."

"I hear it's in response to all those Christians that got away."

"Those Christians they say 'got away' – they didn't get away, they were snatched."

"Snatched? What do you mean?"

"It's a term for an event in the Bible."

"We've all been looking for a Bible but haven't found one – they've been burning those for so many years, I think they're just about all gone."

"It was foretold in the Bible centuries ago that in the End Times, which is the time we are living now, God would rescue the Christians from the earth and bring them to Him. When this happens, some say they are 'snatched', some use the term, 'Raptured'."

"And what about those left behind?" asked Robert. "I have the Mark, but I've come to love the Lord. Maybe bringing us here will mean you'll put a good word in for us," he smiled briefly, and then added, "...I'm serious."

"Maybe the Lord can help you out there," said Mary

"Meaning?"

"Oh, we'll talk about it later after I've had a chance to meet everyone," Mary replied.

"Things look different," said McDee. "Last time we were here the tunnel in front of us was completely open, but now blocked off by those double doors."

"Yes," smiled Allen, "We had to do that 'cause now we have heat! Putting in those doors saves us a lot of hot air – although my wife says I don't need to save no hot air," he smiled.

McDee and Barter did not smile.

"Well, like I said," continued Allen, "we have some talented people. One gentleman we have here worked on building the tunnel. And, along with an engineer and a number of really knowledgeable folks, he has built a hundred small generators powered by water. Next thing you know, we have electricity plus electric heat!"

"Truly amazing," said Roy Kegler. "Truly amazing."

Robert led them out of the central tunnel through the double doors into the heated residential tunnel. As they neared, several of the residents walked out to meet them. There appeared to McDee to be at least double the number of residents now than before. Evidently there were artists included among the new residents – a fact evidenced by the painted murals adorning the curved walls. Each mural was fifteen to twenty feet tall and similar in width. Almost all were of biblical scenes, although a number were drawings of meadows, rivers and other nature scenes.

Vanessa Robertson, another former trooper, greeted them and acted as their guide showing the buildings.

"Yes, we've been busy," smiled Robertson. "Our population has grown and keeping up with it has been a challenge."

"That brings us to why we are here," said Mary. "We are hoping you could find room for us."

Trooper Allen laughed, "Yes, of course. In fact, our guest apartment is now vacant. I'm sure joining our families here will be a wonderful experience for us both."

Mary smiled, "I'm sure it will be."

As they walked, the nearly hundred residents came forward to introduce themselves and their families. This was followed by a tour of a couple of homes. They were nearly identical to homes above ground, except they did not have kitchens. Instead, there were small areas for food storage and snack prep. If one were to stay only in the house one could expect to think they lived in any neighborhood in the country. A number had living rooms, a first-floor bedroom and a couple had second floors with three additional bedrooms.

"From what you've said, it appears you have six separate housing needs. Reverend McDee, can we talk you into living in one of the apartments? We'll show them to you. We have one available right now; they have a living, snack area, and bedroom."

"Sounds perfect to me," smiled McDee

"Okay. That reduces a need to five new homes – actually only three since we have this one and one more we just completed. Some of you can stay in that one until we finish adding new homes."

"Can we take a look at it?"

"Of course – and I think you will find it meets your needs. It's one built with a second floor. It has four bedrooms on the upper level, and a family room on the main level which can easily be converted into a bedroom."

"A family room?"

Miss Allen smiled, "Sounds strange I know, but we wanted the houses to be just like those above ground. In fact, after we began building them, we added the snack areas. After looking over the home, the residents escorted their guests to the dining hall. This was a large structure in the adjacent tunnel, though there was no evidence inside of being a tunnel other than there were no windows. Some of the group gathered around the visitors as Mary sat down while others sought out their own tables. It became very noisy as the many conversations began competing with one another. McDee and others were pleased because the noise was a happy one punctuated with enthusiastic spurts of laughter.

"So, can you bring us any news?" asked Vanessa. One by one the conversations quieted around them as others waited for Mary to answer. The only sounds other than Mary were the cooks preparing the dinner in the kitchen.

"Not really," said Mary. "As we said, we were locked up for a while. Before that, we sorta isolated ourselves and hoped the world – and the Goonies – wouldn't find us."

Allen and Robertson nodded.

"I don't go outside anymore," said Vanessa Robertson. "I decided being out with the police force was too risky – Allen is coming to the same conclusion."

"That's right. Now they are picking out both Marked and Unmarked for execution, one just doesn't know who or when to trust anyone. As far as I can see the executions are pretty much random – especially with the Goonies," said Robertson. "I know the police squad I'm with has been fairly hesitant about picking out people. But, that's about to end. The powers n keeping track of how many 'scores' a unit is able to accumulate on a bi-monthly basis."

"So," broke in Mary, "how do you tell the difference between Christian and Non-Christians when you want to bring someone here?"

Allen shook his head. "We don't have one. Generally, what we do is start asking questions about Bible verses," said Vanessa. "But that's not one hundred percent accurate."

"Any other way?"

"Pray. That's about it. How can we turn people away? We've been praying for an answer 'cause we sure don't want to turn away any sincere Christian."

Tim exchanged looks with Mary. "Well, I think I may have an answer," said Mary slowly and almost in a whisper. Quickly she outlined her life of being blind and of her God-given ability at that time to sense non-Christians and aliens masquerading as humans.

"That's incredible!" voiced Allen

"Well, wait," cautioned Mary. "Then God healed me of my blindness and my abilities to sense and healing faded away."

"I don't think God is all love and kisses," snorted Tim.

111

"Tim! Do you mind?" snapped Mary. "We're having a conversation here among the faithful. If you find that offensive leave!"

Tim snorted again and left the table.

"Your husband isn't a Christian?"

"Yes, he is. He just doesn't want to be. One day he is and the next not. It has to do with a sad time in our lives, but I'm sure he'll find his way back. God won't let him go."

"Do you believe that God took away your abilities because he is punishing you for something?"

"No, of course not, I think he wanted me to learn to use my eyes and other senses to live in a faith relationship. Of course, don't know that's the reason, but that's what I believe. I feel I needed to grow in my faith."

"Pretty faith-driven belief, if you ask me," said Vanessa.

"Well, all this leads me to confess something that has been growing in my heart. I think God has led me here because He's giving me back those abilities."

"Really – you can sense non-Christians?"

"I believe so. There was a non-Christian in our group – he's the reason we were put in jail – or at least so he thought. Anyway, I sensed there was something evil about him, but it was so soft and had been so long that I wasn't sure it had anything to do with my gift."

For a moment everyone was silent, including others at other tables, as they began to tune into the conversation. "But that's not all." Mary's voice betrayed weariness as though what she was about to say stretched her own faith. "Some time ago one of the persons who came with us had the mark."

"She's talking about me," injected Roy Kegler.

"Because of a sudden impulse, I prayed for Roy's mark to leave, and it did."

There were gasps from the surrounding people.

"She's telling the truth!" exclaimed Roy holding up his right hand for all to see. "I didn't feel a thing. One minute I had the Mark and the next it was gone – no feeling at all!"

"I'm not saying I could do it again, but I'm willing to allow God to use me in the effort." Suddenly there was an onslaught of voices volunteering to be the first one.

Mary held up her hands and Roy and McDee joined in an effort to quiet the voices.

"But I want to do this my way. One of the buildings you showed me is used as your chapel?"

"Yes," said Vanessa.

"I want you to select ten people at a time. They will line up in front of the chapel and I will greet each one individually they will go into the church and sit at the rearmost pews. I will call each one up individually."

"And you will remove the Mark?" asked Allen.

"I will do nothing, God removes the Mark."

Silence hung over the group for a minute.

"When?"

Mary smiled. "I understand your impatience, but please, let me do this in my way. I need some time to prepare myself. Tonight, after dinner, Lord willing, we will gather and do this."

Chapter 16: Durk Returns

There was tension in the office. But, there was always tension. Sergeant Sterling wished every minute that went by to be anywhere but here. It was so different than it had been in the past, before there had been jokes and laughter among the office personnel. They had made good-natured jokes about the General, but in truth, they enjoyed serving him. That was the past, however.

Now a cloud hung over their office, in fact, over the entire camp. Since General Valice's death – some whisper it was suicide – no replacement had been appointed. The official story was that it was a home invasion because of the condition of the ransacked house. Also, they said a lot of stuff was missing. Still, the rumor of suicide persisted.

Within a few days, Prefect Durk had taken over command. He and his ever-present black-robed guard were like a breath of bad air. Sterling would sit at his desk nearly paralyzed by the fear of this individual with the red robe in the adjacent office. When he wanted Sterling to come, instead of using the intercom, Durk would send one of the black-robed ones out and motion Sterling to go inside the office.

Entering the office, Sterling would stand at attention until the instructions were over, then exit, without saluting – which Durk found offensive.

Suddenly the door opened, causing Sterling to jump as usual. The black-robed figure motioned for Sterling to go inside Getting up quickly, Sterling went into the office, adjusting his uniform as he did while feeling his stomach turn as fear gripped him. Reaching a spot in front of the desk he came to attention.

"Yes, sir," he said.

The Prefect Durk did not acknowledge his presence, continuing instead to study some papers in front of him. The minutes slowly went by and Sterling wondered if the Prefect

114

had even noticed that he came in. He could feel a bead of sweat trickle from his temple. He was tempted to wipe it, but didn't.

Finally, Durk looked up.

His face was drawn as always and there was no hint of emotion while he studied Sterling.

"Sergeant," he finally said in a low monotone. "I have some disturbing information to share with you."

"Yes, sir," snapped Sterling.

"Captain Bellmore. How well do you know him?"

"Captain Bellmore?" Sterling was at a loss for words. "Not very well, sir. I mean, we have a good working relationship I think. We don't associate off-duty – well, I attended his birthday party a few months ago – he invited me as he did everyone in the office. But that's about it."

"I have some information that Captain Bellmore is not totally committed to our cause. Have you any reason to believe true or not?"

"Uh, well, no sir. I can't say I do. He seems committed as far as I know. In fact, I thought he was very enthusiastic in following orders and trying to advance."

Durk nodded silently. "Well, impressions can be misleading." Durk reached down and opened the side drawer of his desk. Slowly he withdrew a forty-five caliber pistol and laid it on the edge of the desk with the handle facing Sterling.

Sterling was shocked by the motion and stared at the gun without a guess as to what it meant, other than he was sure it didn't bode well.

"I've sent word for Captain Bellmore to come to the office." He nodded to the black-robed alien who opened the door motioning to Bellmore. Bellmore came in, and if he was surprised to see Sterling, he gave no indication. Coming to a spot next to Sterling, he assumed a similar position of ridged attention.

Durk stared at Bellmore who was obviously nervous even though there wasn't any action indicating it other than the slight irregular quivering of his bottom lip.

Turning his attention to Sterling, he nodded at the gun. "Sergeant I want you to pick up the gun. Be careful how you handle it – it's loaded."

Carefully Sterling reached down and gathered the gun in his right hand, pointing it at the floor.

"Captain Bellmore," said Durk, "I have some information that you are not following my orders. In fact, I believe you have even made some comments that you do not believe in our cause."

Bellmore gasped slightly. "No, sir. That's not true; I've supported you and followed every order given me."

"Captain, if I told you I could see your soul – would you believe me?"

"My... my soul?"

Durk nodded.

"Well, I don't understand. What do you mean soul? I thought the message was we did not have a soul. I don't understand."

"It makes no difference, I was just curious," said Durk. Then turning his attention to Sterling, he said, "Sergeant, because we have made the judgment that Captain Bellmore is not entirely loyal to us, it is my judgment that he should be eliminated, and my command to you now is to take that pistol and shoot Captain Bellmore."

"Sir?"

"You heard me, Sergeant."

"But sir, I can't do that."

"Sergeant, if you don't want me to think you are disloyal too, you will do as I command."

Sterling stood staring at Durk, then at Bellmore who was now clearly dripping with sweat, though remaining at Attention. Slowly, Sterling brought the gun up to his waist where he stared at it for several minutes with the room remaining absolutely silent. Then, coming to a resolve, pointed the gun at Durk and pulled the trigger.

* * * * *

Tim followed her silently as she left the eating area. She was deep in thought and Tim knew she was burdened by the wishes of those in camp, but also by himself and his attitude. They walked to the apartment with the twins trailing. Entering, Mary did not stop but went straight to their bedroom. Tim hesitated to follow her and motioned to the twins to stop. Perhaps his hesitancy was the chasm which had developed between them. He had to tell Mary his feelings and make things right.

Entering the bedroom, he slowly closed the door behind him. Mary was sitting on the bed staring at the floor and did not acknowledge Tim's presence.

"What's the matter?" he asked.

Mary looked up giving a small smile. "Nothing is wrong; I'm just trying to gather my faith together for what lies ahead. I don't want to disappoint these people, and I don't want to fail God."

"You won't fail. God is with you. That brings me to what I want to tell you." Tim knelt before his wife. "Honey," he said softly. "I'm sorry – I'm so sorry." The last words came out overcome with emotion. Tim paused as he gathered himself. "How could I be so self-centered? Can you forgive me?"

Mary gave a small smile and gently stroked his hair. "Of course, and get up before you get your pants all dirty."

Tim smiled and sat beside her, softly stroking her hair as they embraced. "I've been so angry about the baby," he said.

"I know, I know. I've had a tough time with it too. You're angry with God, I understand. What we have to realize is that we have flesh, bone, and blood all around our soul and it sometimes gets in the way of our connection with Him. In keeping a connection of faith, sometimes our soul has to fight through our human emotions, our desires, our fears, occasionally even our anger with Him. And, when that happens, it takes time."

"Yet," replied Tim, "you haven't let it get in the way of your own faith. I think, for a little time, it destroyed my faith in God."

"I understand. You aren't any different than anyone else, Tim. We all need to struggle at times to keep or grow our faith. It isn't always easy. I knew, in time, you would feel God's touch on you."

"I see how loving He is, yet I couldn't understand why our baby didn't live. I will never understand. Never, until I am face to face with Him, and He tells me why. But, you – your faith has made me understand I can wait, and I can serve. I can serve you, too."

Mary pulled away. "Don't say that – you do not serve me! Together we serve God. You are and always will be the head of our household. I depend on you to be my rock."

There was a soft knock at the door, before opening slowly. The twins came in smiling. "We're a little hungry and Mr. Allen said they are having hamburgers tonight." Mary and Tim looked at each other.

"Well, I think we're a little hungry, too," smiled Tim. "Why don't we all go and have one of those yummy burgers?" Mary and Tim took the hands of the twins and began walking to the Dining Hall.

"Can we sit with the other kids?" asked Alison.

Mary smiled, "Sure, I think that would be fun, but when Tim and I get ready to go we need you to get up and come with us – no begging, okay?"

"Oh, look!" squealed Alison as she pointed to the sky. "I just saw a shooting star."

"Oh, there's another," shouted Tim.

Then there came a number of them, some just quick streaks, and others lasting until nearly hitting earth.

"Oh, Tim, look," said Mary.

A large streak of a meteor came across the sky much larger than any before. Bits and pieces flew off as it traversed the sky. "I'll bet that one hit someplace," Tim said.

Mary nodded. "I saw a meteor like that before, a while back. It was not natural."

"Not... you mean you think this one is somehow evil?"

Mary thought for a moment. "I think we should keep it in mind. Maybe it was just a natural show by nature, but it's possible it was something more."

Tim nodded as they started walking again. They were soon joined by others on their way to the Dining Hall. Inside there were several long tables each capable of seating ten to fifteen people. The noise was almost deafening as everyone seemed in a chatty mood. Tim noticed no one approached Mary with any questions about what she was going to do for them that night, and he mentioned that fact to Mary.

"Oh, I think they probably don't know what to say or ask," smiled Mary.

The dinner was delicious consisting of a small hamburger (a rare treat), a salad without dressing and a small portion of potatoes. People who wished could go back for seconds as long as the food lasted. The seating, serving, and eating took the best part of the hour.

Tim noticed as the time went on, the noisy conversations diminished. More and more, he saw people stealing glances at Mary as she slowly ate her dinner and chatted with the twins and Betty. Finally, the entire mess hall was silent, a fact that escaped Mary's notice until in mid-sentence, she stopped and looked around at the faces watching her. For a second, she was stunned, but then a smile emerged on her face, followed by growing laughter. Her laugh was infectious and soon the entire mess hall was filled with laughter.

Mary slowly got up with her party and made her way to the chapel. Behind them followed the first ten people selected by the group along with the others trailing. How or when they had been selected Tim or Mary didn't know, but they were certainly unchallenged.

Arriving at the chapel, Mary stopped and the ten stopped behind her.

Turning, Mary spoke with a raised voice. "Please, get in a single line."

Immediately a line formed, and Mary began walking slowly along it. To each, she smiled and gave a greeting while briefly holding their hand. Finishing, she walked back to Tim.

"I didn't feel anything that made me think they weren't sincere."

Tim nodded.

Mary went into the chapel as Tim motioned the others to follow. Inside Margie and Betty directed them to the rear bench they were to occupy.

Tim caught up to Mary as she approached the altar. There, he went to the side retrieving a roughly crafted bench and brought it to the center. Placing it behind her, he waited as Mary prayed at the altar. Finally turning, she sat on the bench motioning the first individual to come up.

The first she recognized as Vanessa Robertson who seemed very nervous and was rubbing the palms of her hands on her legs as she approached.

"Vanessa, please kneel here," smiled Mary. "And don't be nervous, that's my job."

Gently she took Vanessa's right hand and held it between both of her own. Then closing her eyes, she remained silent few moments. Finally, she opened her eyes and looked at Vanessa. "Vanessa, do you believe that Jesus Christ is the Son of God Almighty?"

"I do."

"Do you believe that He is the door through which we must go to reach God's eternal kingdom?"

"I do."

Again, Mary was silent, closing her eyes for a few moments. Then, opening her eyes, she smiled, "God loves you, Van – welcome to his chosen Kingdom." Releasing her hand Vanessa looked down at the back of his right hand. She screamed joy, jumping up and showing everyone, her hand was as fresh as the day she was born, without blemish – or the Mark. The hushed audience burst into their own screams and hoots with shouts of 'Praise God!' and 'Thank you, Jesus!'" From outside, there came more shouts as they heard and knew what the celebratory noise meant. There was a renewed celebration when Vanessa ran out showing them her hand.

Then one by one each came forward and the scene was repeated. The celebration never seemed to grow old as each saw the Mark was indeed gone. Outside there was laughter and shouts of praise. Finally, they broke into song, singing Amazing Grace over and over.

As the last one ran out the door, Tim approached his wife. "You look exhausted."

Mary nodded, smiling.

Chapter 17: Evil Revealed

The bullet exploded from the muzzle of Sterling's gun causing Durk's robe to jump followed by a dull thump as it burrowed into the back of the chair. Durk stared unmoved at Sterling who was frozen, still pointing the gun. Sterling pulled the trigger and again there was a deafening sound followed by the clothes jumping and the thump.

The door behind Sterling and Bellmore suddenly snapped shut on its own and the lock clicked just in time to prevent the clerks from the outer office rushing into the room.

Durk smiled. "I think you have made a big mistake, Sergeant Sterling." His voice was calm and low with a trace of amusement.

Sterling stared at Durk. "It's true. It's true!" he gasped. "You aren't flesh and blood – You're the devil! Everything the Fanatics have been saying is true!" His voice grew in volume as the realization exploded in his mind and his soul.

"Oh, Sergeant Sterling, compliments will get you nowhere," grinned Durk. "I am not the Devil. No, nor am I the great Heylel. I cannot but submit my all to the great Abaddon. I am not even the master Abdon, or one of the Lords of Belial, or Cerberus nor of the Legion or Python. I am just doing my duty, like you."

Durk slowly rose from his chair and, while straightening his robe, came casually around the desk. Reaching the front, and facing the two soldiers, he leaned back and folded his arms.

"What's going on here?" asked Captain Bellmore.

"Don't you understand, you idiot!" snapped Sterling.

"How dare you call me that! I'll have you demoted!" said Bellmore who, for the first time, showed some animation. He turned back to Durk. "Are you wearing a bulletproof vest? What is this some kind of gigantic joke? We are the United

States Army headquarters, not some beer joint!" Bellmore's voice grew in strength until he was shouting.

Suddenly Durk's left hand shot out grabbing Bellmore by the throat, lifting him off the ground. Bellmore struggled but only succeeded in a tight gurgle as the hand tightened around his neck. He began desperately trying to pry Durk's fingers apart while his feet began kicking.

"Let him go!" shouted Sterling as he joined in trying to pry Durk's finger loose. Durk reached out with his right-hand grabbing Sterling's throat and holding both men above the floor.

Outside the office, the two Corporals began banging on the door while shouting to gain entrance. Finally, they heard a click and the door swung open slowly. Taken aback for a moment, they hesitated before rushing inside. Once inside, they found bodies of both Captain Bellmore and Sergeant Sterling inert on the floor.

"What's happening, sir?" shouted the first Sergeant.

"I'm sorry to report these two men were sympathizers for the Freaks. We had no choice but to pass sentence upon them. Contact the proper unit and have the bodies removed."

For a moment, both soldiers remained in shocked silence; but recovering, gave a quick, "Yes, sir!"

Durk, followed by his two escorts, left the office. The two soldiers remained silent for a moment after the outer door closed, then turned to each other.

"What the hell is going on?" the first whispered.

The second lifted his finger to his lips imploring the other to be quiet. Then looked up and pointed while saying, "You never know. These poor slobs probably got what they deserved." Again, he pointed to the ceiling.

The other nodded in understanding.

As Durk walked down the hallway he turned to the robed figures behind him. "I will contact Abdon and ask him to come here. We need to gather the District Commissioners of this country. I want this area of the country to be the most effective of all the districts. Obviously, there are more dirty God people here than first estimated."

"Yes, Prefect, but Abdon just met with them in the Pyramid."

Durk stopped short, "Are you questioning my decisions?"

The robed escort bowed. "Of course not, Prefect Durk."

"I think they are losing focus on the mission. We must re-instill in them how harmful the Christians and Jews have been. Too many of the District Commissioners are letting the Goonies do the dirty work while they sit in their quarters. I think they have forgotten the harm these religious fanatics are doing to our cause. We have to convince these filthy humans they should already be on their way to the stars, and here they are mired in this dirty game of sparing humans."

"We will bring them here Prefect."

"I also want some Christian humans to be there also, including some marked ones. I think it may be very important all District Commissioners understand, from their own kind, that it is this lingering filthy business of Christianity that is holding us back."

"We will make it so, Prefect."

Durk stopped and looked around at the empty hallway. "Tell me, has Abdon's special surprise been released here yet?

"Yes Prefect, they have already been released in the Prefect area of Europe. Some have come here to what they call Americas – to the North. I have been told it will find its way to your area within the coming weeks."

Durk nodded. "Oh, and another thing, when we have the District Commissioners gathered I want to be able to demonstrate this District is tracking down these Christians. Has that Christian police officer been tracked to where his band of Christians are hiding?"

"Yes, sir, I was going to tell you. We received word that he has been tracked to some kind of forest station in the hills."

"What are you talking about – I don't want some station, I want Christians!" His voice rose until it echoed on the halls.

"Yes, sir, of course. The Christians are hiding next to the forest station in a large underground warehouse affair."

"So how many are there?"

"We don't know exactly, but we estimate between twenty and a hundred."

"Twenty? There better be more than twenty! If that's all there is, you are wasting time and energy, and you will have to answer for that. Wait, do they have our Mark?"

"Yes."

"Excellent. At least we can make up for numbers by showing how the 'marked ones' are hiding. They will make good examples for our assembly of District Commissioners."

"Yes, we are ready to move on them at your command."

Durk nodded, a small rare smile on his dark image.

* * * * *

During these times it was rare that a day, let alone several, was peaceful. Yet, so it was now for those living in Camp New Adam. All the officers, other than Robert Allen, and a couple of others who helped him, had ceased going out of the tunnel except for specific items the group needed, including material for the new escape tunnel. It was Mary's suggestion to find some way to create an escape tunnel. Several of the men had decided to take on the project, including Tim. Their efforts resulted in creating a hole in the main structure approximately one mile from the living quarters. Care had to be taken in cutting an opening since they wanted it large enough to walk through, yet not compromise the strength of the structure. In addition to the delicate task of cutting the opening, they had to excavate the dirt. Using the smaller cement castings originally intended as tributaries, they excavated another, though much smaller tunnel, leading away to an area outside that would allow them to exit without detection. The height of the cement castings was high enough, so most could walk through, while others simply had to lower their head.

It took almost six weeks, but finally it was completed. The entire population of the camp journeyed to the new tunnel which ran westward away from the main tunnels, exiting onto a small creek running north and south. The creek then ran for several miles in either direction fed by groundwater emptying to the north in another small river.

The area where the creek ran was part of several farms' acreages. The shores of the creek were left undisturbed by the farmers for approximately twenty feet on either side. They now provided a pleasant mini forest through which the creek and the residents walked. The surrounding, once prosperous farms now lay fallow, and tall weeds had begun to grow everywhere.

Several of the residents had begun to clear patches in the weeds in preparation for plantings. It was thought that the remote location and height of weeds would hide small gardens.

On the days when the air was cleaner than others, some began using the tunnel to venture out and use the creek bank for picnics. Tim and Mary and the twins began to be among the more frequent walkers along the creek.

On this day's walk, as on most, Mary and the girls would take off their shoes and walk in the shallow waters. Tim would walk on the shore, laughing as he teased, saying he saw huge snakes in the water. But, that didn't work anymore, as the girls told him they saw bears behind him. Today, Mary came to the river bank and sat down with Tim while the girls started hunting for pretty rocks in the water.

"Tell me, Mary, what's ahead? Do you know anything that is going to happen?"

Mary smiled, "Oh, I'm not a fortune teller – I don't know exactly what's going to happen. I think some tough times are ahead, and I'm getting the feeling it involves us traveling."

"Really. We are going to be moving?"

"Oh, I can't say that for sure, but I get that sense. One thing that has been bothering me is the bus. I think parking it outside the forest station invites scrutiny."

"Do you think we might have someone coming here that would be curious or recognize it? I can't remember anyone dropping by that forest station since we moved here."

Mary nodded. "Yes, but I just think we should move it."

"Where?"

"I was thinking we could bring it across the old farmer's tractor path back there and park it under the trees," said Mary pointing across the way. "I don't think it could be seen, and even if it could, no one would connect it with us."

"Sounds good."

For a moment, they both watched the twins running back and forth in the water with excited screams as they tried to catch small fish.

"You should be very proud of yourself, Tim," said Mary. "You've brought these wonderful girls through some of the most dangerous years in human history."

Tim remained silent, looking at the girls in the water.

Mary could see tears filling his eyes and knew their source.

"Now honey, I know Mickey didn't make it," she said referring to the wonderful, joy-filled boy who was murdered back at Camp Noah.

Tim nodded, choking back his tears. Taking a deep breath, he brought his grief under control. "I can't stop thinking about him. He trusted me to take care of him, and I didn't."

"That's not true, and you know it!" snapped Mary. "He was killed by an evil man, and there was nothing you could have done about it." Mary stopped short, and then leaned forward. "That's where it began, didn't it? You're holding Mickey's death against God, aren't you?"

Tim looked at Mary; his expression was no longer vulnerable, but hard. "No, that's not where it began. It started

127

back our church when I came up and saw all those people dead. And then... I saw my parents with their right hands cut off."

"That must have been terrible," said Mary.

Tim nodded. "But I didn't let myself absorb it too much; I knew I had to get the kids out of there. I didn't know what was going to happen, and finding the camp was so lucky."

"And is that what you believe, it was 'lucky'?"

Tim ignored the comment. "Then when Mickey was killed, it just got piled on top of my losing my parents. And then... then, there was our baby," he said in a whisper.

Both were silent for a few minutes until Mary spoke. "I won't pretend, honey that I know about the grief of losing your parents. I do not, both my parents are here and healthy, but I do know the grief of losing a child. And I'll say this: Your grief cannot match the loss suffered by a mother."

From the creek, Alison yelled, "Watch me!" She then kneeled and, holding her nose, put her face under the water for a second or two. Then stood up sputtering and coughing as though near death.

Both Tim and Mary clapped and smiled. The two girls then lay on the stomachs and pretended to swim.

"I've tried hard – and believe me when I say this Mary – I've tried so hard to believe God is in charge of everything and those deaths were for a greater good. I've tried, I just can't."

"I don't think God expects you to do that, Tim. I wish I could tell you the 'whys' and 'wherefores' of all that occurs in the world, or even what happens to us. I can't. I know sometimes I sound like a broken record, but not knowing is how we learn faith. It's sorrow that is the fertile ground of joy just as fear births courage. It is the darkness which makes us love light. Through our sorrows, we learn the treasures of joy." Mary paused for a moment before continuing.

"I believe God set out the rules for all that exists, including us. They were set out to provide us an everlasting life of joy. Satan has manipulated those rules to his favor and because of it turned much of the joys to sorrow. However, every victory Satan has claimed has been turned to God's favor. For it is through our sorrow that the mercies of God can be shown, though not necessarily explained."

Tim nodded. "Yes, I know you are right. There was a time when I would have cursed what you are saying, but now I don't. I know it's true. I know that I will meet the souls of my parents, and Mickey, and so many others in a joyous reunion. I know this because of you. Mary, you have led me to my faith," he smiled. "I think of it as a reunion." They both laughed and kissed as they heard the girls coming out of the water.

Those were peaceful days for Mary, Tim, and the twins. Quiet times spent as a family along with all the others living in the village inside of a tunnel. In fact, many called it Tunnel Village, and all were constantly engaged in making it as attractive as they could. Peaceful days below, while above the ash, though lighter, still darkened the sun and cooled the air. Hundreds of thousands contracted breathing disorders; however, because there were so many closed hospitals and secluded doctors, so many perished.

However, the peaceful days came to an end when Trooper Allen came back one day from work with news. The resident knew something was wrong when Allen drove down the entrance into the tunnel rather than parking his cruiser at the station.

Stopping the car, Allen immediately ran to the Gathering House where he knew most would be during the late afternoon.

"Bad News," he blurted out as he arrived. "We got an epidemic headed our way!"

"Epidemic?" asked Mary. "What do you mean?"

"Some weird disease that they don't know how to stop. Seems it started in Europe a few months ago and made its way here. Word is hundreds of thousands have died in Europe."

"How did you find out?"

129

"At the station, they got word through police bands," replied Allen. "They say it's already in the New England states and headed west and south."

"They don't know the name of the disease?" asked Betty.

"At first, they thought it was smallpox, then Typhus, Yellow Fever, Anthrax, Glanders – whatever that is, and some others I can't pronounce, but nothing matches exactly. And – and get this, they haven't found anything to cure it nor a vaccine to prevent it!"

"How is it transmitted?" asked Mary.

"They don't even know – they don't even know when people contract it. Everybody feels fine, until one day they start vomiting blood. From that time to death is only a couple of days! The closest they've come to identifying it is through autopsies. Somehow it gets into the blood, but they haven't been able to tell was 'it' is exactly. Once in the blood seems to nest in the stomach and literally eats it up. The first indication the patient has the bug, or whatever, is an upset stomach but by that time it's too late."

For a moment Mary was silent as she stared at the floor. Finally, she took a deep breath. "I don't think anyone will find a cure for this disease. I feel we are missing something. I need to have time with the Lord.

Reverend McDee put his hand on Mary's shoulder. "You can count on all of us for our prayers."

"There's something else. Something else is going to happen, but I'm not clear what yet. I believe we are nearing a change."

Mary paused and looked around at the crowd of people who were watching her expectantly. "But I know this, God is with us."

Chapter 18: Prefects All

Three weeks later, amid private grumblings, the District Commissioners assembled for their meeting with the Regional Prefect Durk and Abdon. The Arbitrage Hotel in Charlotte was chosen to host the meeting. Despite the fast-growing unemployment all around, the Arbitrage managed to hang on to more employees than expected. It was attributed to the hotel's opening a number of rooms to its employees free of charge as permanent living quarters. Though that significantly reduced number of rooms available for guests – there weren't a large number of guests these days

Abdon was escorted into the meeting room by Durk, accompanied by four robed escorts. Seated around the horseshoe-arranged tables were the thirteen commissioners, except for Durk who remained standing with Abdon, facing the podium. The chatter abruptly ceased with Abdon's entrance, and the silence seemed to grow, as he faced the group from the podium.

"I welcome you here," he began in his low, almost guttural tone, while casting a slow examining eye around the table. "Prefect Durk has asked me to come here because he feels you have lost focus of the purpose you are to serve." There was a slight stirring.

"Some time ago I addressed you, explaining that our mission here is to rescue you from the menaces that are now starting to befall this planet. These are only the first of many as the Earth begins to die. Do you understand – this planet is dying!" His voice rose until hurting ears to hear it. "If you have no concern for the people of your planet, what about your own families and yourself? No one will be allowed to escape until all the religious fanatics are dead. What part of that do you not understand!" Abdon fell silent, as if trying to compose himself while examining the commissioners. Several squirmed as his penetrating gaze seemed to reach inside them. They avoided exchanging looks with him, averting their eyes as they found themselves under his penetrating gaze.

"I think you have allowed those you call Goonies to do your work for you. Commissioner Durk is concerned that soon you may give up entirely in the cleansing. That you might be content, feeling you do not need to do anything on your own. Don't fall into this trap. If you do, you shall be your own victim, for such behavior will be looked upon as disloyal and will result in these Last Days your own public execution!"

The room was absolutely silent.

Abdon's tone softened as he continued. "Now, we understand your troops have some hesitancy about executing fellow citizens. It is not only true with your Districts, it is true all over the world – we understand that; however, the fact still remains, this cleansing of your people must be done."

Abdon turned, motioning Durk to step forward.

"Your Prefect, who besides his regional responsibilities has assumed command of District 5, is using initiative which is what we need in all Districts. Prefect, tell us about today's example."

Durk stepped forward, removing his hood as he did. "We have been sending out patrols searching for nests of the religious fanatics, but also we have been examining our own troops. Recently, because of this examination, we found one of our police officers was a secret Christian, even though he bore our Mark." There was a low but brief noise from the audience.

"Yes, as some of you suspected, that is the new tactic of these abominable Christians. They are now putting a fake mark on themselves, so they may hide among us. I'm sure you are aware of all the Christians who've disappeared – well, this is your answer. They are not gone; they're among your people, walking around as they please!" Again, there was some brief murmuring.

"Now, regarding the police officer, I directed that they monitor this officer's movements and it has resulted in our locating is a fairly large group of religious fanatics living in an old water tunnel construction."

"Have you captured them yet?" The question came from General Damon of District One.

"Patience – you sound like my men," he smiled. "No, not yet, we are preparing the troops as we speak. We have made sure that none of our men are anywhere around the target area so we don't tip them about our intentions. But soon we will move."

The meeting dragged on for another half hour before the robed aliens, including Durk, left the quiet room. For a few moments the silence lingered, before finally soft conversations began among the commissioners.

"Did you catch the threat he made?" asked General Damon. "We better come up with some body counts, or our own will be one of them."

General Trombley slapped his fist on the table, startling a few. "Is that what we've become? Little lap dogs to these guys – not that I'm really complaining," he added as he looked around the room. "But I'm, ah, disturbed that my efforts are being questioned. I understand the Goonies are not popular people, but in my District, they've accounted for over 20,000 executions – what's so bad about that?"

There were mutters of agreement around the table. General Kaake of the eleventh district held out his hand. "What procedures have any of you developed to decide which of the Marked people are Christians faking it, and which are dedicated to the Cause?"

The table remained silent until Colonel Cole spoke up. "Well, I just told my people to look into their eyes and see if they avert their view."

"Wouldn't a lot of people do that?" asked Kaake.

Cole nodded. "And that's why, despite our low population, our western district has over 45,000 kills to date. I think you saw at the last posting we were second in all the nation and fifteenth in the world," Cole said proudly. Then, lowering his tone, "I don't send them out too much anymore."

"And why is Durk bragging about going to kill a hundred Christians – what's so big about that?" asked Trombley.

"Because anything he does is a big deal. You wanna be a big deal? Get a black robe," chuckled Tucker.

The rest muttered their agreement as they rose and left the room.

* * * * *

This day was one of the more unusual with the sky showing patches of blue, allowing the summer sun to peek through. The result was a number of families going outside, both to the front, by the station, and others out the escape passage by the river. Most of the families going to the river walked to the north, where the river bank was wide and flat. For this reason, Mary and Tim, along with the twins, walked to the south wanting some alone time.

They walked in silence, both enjoying the feel of the warm sun and the peace of the day. They nodded to the few who had chosen to walk this same direction, but eventually were alone.

"So, honey, what do you think is ahead?"

Mary breathed deeply before speaking. "I don't wanna talk about that today. I just want to think about now and about happy hour with you."

Tim smiled, taking his wife's hand and then raising it for a kiss. The two continued in silence for the next few moments until Mary spoke. "Do you remember Andy Moore's wedding?" she smiled. "He was in that suit that was split up the back and around the shoulders," she laughed out loud.

Tim laughed, "I remember watching him and Stephanie walking out. It looked like he'd just been in a fight – and lost. They both started laughing harder than they had in a long time. Each time they began to stop, just a look at the other sent them into convulsions of laughter again.

"Yeah, when you think back on it, we all have led such a life in the past few years. Before coming to camp, I recall having to rob convenience stores for food to feed the kids. I was sure I would be caught. I don't mind admitting I was scared every time. 'Course the kids loved it. We had those two-ways and they would play with them just when I was sweating bullets. Especially the girls, they were the giggly ones – but Mickey loved it. He like playing lookout, and spy and soldier and ..." Tim's voice trailed off and Mary allowed the silence to grow for a moment before speaking.

"You cared for him so well, no one could have asked for a better daddy."

Tim squeezed her hand. They continued in silence for a minute.

"I remember the first time I saw you," said Tim softly.

"Oh, really?" Mary said coyly.

"Yes, I thought you were really good looking," Tim smiled

"Really?"

"Umm–hmm."

"Like a movie star?" asked Mary her voice rising slowly at the end.

"Well, I think you're trying to milk this a little."

"So, you're done?"

"Think so," smiled Tim.

"Those were good times, honey," said Mary as she nestled her head on his shoulder and drew closer.

"Those were the best days of my life. When I met you, I just knew that you were the one – I just knew it. I didn't know what you looked like, but I sensed your heart."

"So, did you ask anyone what I looked like?"

135

"Yes, just about everyone."

"And?"

"They all said you were handsome."

"And now that you can see me, do you agree?"

"Oh, yes."

"Like a movie star?"

Mary stepped back and slapped him on the shoulder as she smiled.

Suddenly, Mary grabbed Tim's arm. "Wait," she said.

Some seventy-five yards ahead was a fisherman engrossed in the line he had in the water.

"Tim, would you mind going back to the camp? I think I know who this might be, and I need some alone time with him."

"What are you talking about? I'm not going to leave you out here by yourself."

"Please?"

For a moment Tim hesitated, giving another look to the fisherman, then nodded. "It's him isn't it?"

"I think so."

He leaned over to his wife and they exchanged a kiss.

For a minute Mary watched her husband and the two girls walk away, and then turned towards the fisherman. At first, she began trotting towards him, but as she neared it became a slow walk. He had on a blue wool overcoat which seemed excessive considering the pleasant temperature. Approaching him, she cleared her throat but he gave no indication he was aware of her.

"Hello, Andy," she said. "Catch anything?"

Slowly the man turned. "Hello Mary. No, I'm afraid they aren't biting today," he smiled.

"It's so good to see you; can I give you a hug?"

"I think that would be nice."

Mary sank to her knees wrapping her arms around the Prophet, hugging him around his shoulders. As she did, a short sob escaped her lips.

"Now, don't cry Mary," Andy said softly.

She paused for a moment before speaking again. "Oh Andy, I don't know what to do," she managed between stifled tears.

"Well, that's why I'm here," he said while adjusting the barren string in the water. "I think you need a little help."

"Oh, I do. Everyone is always asking me 'What should we do? When? Why? How?' Oh, Andy, I just don't know the answers."

"I know you don't."

"But everyone expects that I do."

"Mary I've been there – believe me, I've been there."

"But you seemed to know so much."

"I had help. You know the Hermit? He's an angel – did you know that?"

Mary shook her head slowly. "I wondered at times, but I didn't know."

"Yep, a certified angel. 'Course I didn't know it at the time. I just thought he was a crazy ol' man that knew a lot. But always leading me, suggesting I consider this and that. I tell you it drives one crazy. What we need are answers, right? We need someone to say, 'Do this, Do that'."

"Exactly!" exclaimed Mary.

"But you know as well as I do why they don't."

"Faith," said Mary in a low unenthusiastic voice.

Andy laughed. "Well, don't sound so down about it."

"Oh, I didn't mean to, it's just that I need answers so bad – I need help!"

"Now, there's a word that can get some action. It can even bring a lousy fisherman into your life," he smiled. "The answers are what we are supposed to discover, and help is something that points us towards those answers. Sometimes what happens doesn't even look like help. It could even mean tragedies in our lives, or hardship – sometimes things happen that seem to prove God doesn't care, or doesn't love us. But this is not true. We shouldn't let our eternal soul be deceived by the day's events. We are on a journey of endless days, not just one."

Mary was silent for a moment, before speaking. "I get these feelings that I should be doing something, or that something is about to happen – but I don't know what. All these people's lives rely on my knowing – and I don't."

"God knows that; it's why I'm here. All Christians know that the catastrophes which are befalling the Earth were predicted centuries ago and written in the God's book."

"I know, I know. I don't reject God's judgments; I just need to know I'm doing the right thing. When God did not take us, when He snatched all others, I decided it was because He had a mission for us. I believe now that task – and I assume there are many, many like us – is to help unite those left behind who have been deceived and now have turned to Christ."

"Yes."

"But I am failing. There are only a little over one hundred souls with me while there are millions who have not been reached."

"There will be more – a lot more. God will guide you, as He is guiding thousands of others all over the world; however, this is in the future. First, I must share something with you: as we speak there are forces being gathered to arrest and execute you here. You must gather your people and leave for the north."

"How much time do we have?"

"That I don't know, I'm just aware that it will be soon. Mary, let God do His work. He will show you when, what, and where. There are more people who God speaks to than just you. He will bring others to you and bring you to others."

Mary nodded, trying to take a deep breath to settle her panic down.

"There is something else. You have learned of the disease that is coming?"

"Yes!" exclaimed Mary. "We just heard about it! "

138

"This is not natural. This is Satan's doing. Some time ago there was a bright star that fell to the earth."

"Are you talking about the meteor shower?"

"Yes, does it bring anything to mind?"

Mary thought for a moment, then her eyes brighten, "Oh my lord, I hadn't thought of it before – I mean the connection God's Word."

Andy nodded.

"Revelations," said Mary. "I think around the Ninth"

"Yes, the Ninth."

"But I haven't heard any reports of locusts – I mean mass amounts of locusts."

"They are called locusts, but they are very small, very, very small – do you understand?"

Mary nodded slowly. "Like microscopic?"

Andy nodded. "And they appear as they are described in God's Word."

Mary eyes widened, "As in viruses!"

"Yes, I don't want to get technical – because I never was. But I'm told it's called a T-Even Bacteriophage consisting of a head, body and winged tail. I suppose in ancient times it looked like a weird locust. Their service to Satan in the Last Days was foretold in Revelations – but fear not. Because this is of Satan, it will not infect those who are under the protection of Christ. You know he is out to destroy all of mankind, not just Christians. This is another way Satan is out to exterminate mankind."

Mary nodded and silent for a moment as she thought about the implications of all The Prophet had told her.

"Thank you," she said finally.

"Don't thank me I'm just the messenger – why I can't even catch fish."

Mary smiled as she watched Andy pull his branch and string up and lay it beside him.

"Maybe they just aren't biting," he smiled.

As Andy stood Mary gave him a lasting hug. "Thank you, Andy."

Andy smiled, nodded, then began walking down the stream, and as did, faded away.

Chapter 19: The Journey

Mary didn't recognize the scene; however, it certainly was pleasing. Her early childhood had been spent on a farm west of Asheville, and this reminded her of those days. There was the green grass flowing over the slightly rounded hills, the rib fences rising and falling with the rolling terrain along with a slight smell of wheat in the air. For some reason she expected horses to be in the lush fields.

Suddenly, feeling an unexpected bump, she let out a short cry of surprise. Looking down, realized she was on a horse and it was walking. The horse's uneven gate gave a bumpy ride, not at all pleasant. She nudged the horse, as though she was an experienced rider, and the horse broke into an easy cantor which smoothed out the ride. It was almost pleasant. On one hand, she felt relaxed, yet on the other, disturbed because she'd never ridden a horse in her life. Nevertheless, she felt good, at ease and, well, joyful.

From behind, she saw a sword. It was bigger than even the horse she was on and it was gaining upon her. Beneath the sword was an almost invisible horse. The horse's spittle flying off in the wind as it was in full gallop towards her. Instinctively she heeled her horse and it began running, but not fast enough as the sword and its pale horse was gaining. She kicked the horse and hung on to the main as the horse broke into a full-out gallop.

Looking back, the sword was still gaining, though not nearly as much. Then, out of the tip of the sword, came the face of a creature she knew was evil. It was staring at her with eyes that seemed to penetrate her soul, and the intense expression of the face looked as if he thought her a delicious meal.

"Ahhh!" she cried, jerking to a sitting position in bed. Breathing deeply, she tried to keep her emotions in check.

"What is it honey?" asked Tim.

Mary shook her head, "Just a dream."

"Here," said Tim sitting up and resting against the headboard. "You come here, and lean against me. I'll hold you and nothing will get you. How about that?"

Mary turned and smiling accepted the invitation.

"Why don't you tell me about it?"

Mary shook her head. "Not yet, I've got to think."

"Okay, I understand," he said. He'd come to know when his wife's dreams were and were not important. Evidently, she felt this was something special.

Mary sat back and thought about the dream. There was a time in her life when her dreams were either great entertainment or frightening, but they meant nothing beyond that. It was different now. From the time she regained her sight, and now some other lost abilities, her dreams often seem to mean something beyond nightly entertainment. She'd learned there was a difference between those adventures of the mind as she slept, and those times when she was receiving a message.

She tried to explain the difference to Tim, but it proved to be too difficult. There was a different feel to the dreams, a difference in their depth. But, most of all, the response of her soul, and that was the tip-off, the response of her soul. It took a long time to realize the difference, to trust the feeling. Tonight, she was convinced this was not a dream of entertainment – the angels trying to tell her something.

She took a deep breath trying to clear her mind. There had been the sword, but it wasn't an ordinary sword, it was damaged as though in many battles. It was worn, not shiny, and from it had come a face, which she knew was evil – clearly, this old, worn sword was the source of his power.

It occurred to her that she may have seen this sword before. Could it be that this was the sword of Revelation? Was the face she saw, the face of the fourth angel, the Angel of Death?

She thought about the horse. It was without any defined color to it, almost ethereal in its – appearance. Suddenly, it connected. It was the pale horse of Revelations.

Mary concentrated upon the scene to see if there was something she missed. The ethereal form of the horse was trailed by many dim figures. The more she concentrated upon the figures, she realized there were many of them and they were wearing strange clothing that looked like leaves... no, not leaves! Camouflage! They were soldiers! They were coming!

* * * * *

Sergeant Brunswick looked over the assembled men. Being promoted to First Sergeant suited him well. True, it meant giving up command in the field for a desk job, but that had its privileges. Normally he would not be out here this night assembling troops; he'd be in his bed. But this was special, and he'd insisted to his superior that he should be here. It was, in a sense, his gig.

If Prefect Durk's orders were followed, they would be in the trucks soon and on their way. He was growing impatient with the delay and was about to seek out the reason for it when the order was given to mount the trucks. There were twenty vehicles in this convoy, and another twenty were coming directly from Asheville. They were scheduled to deploy near the abandoned water tunnels at three in the morning. Until then the area was kept vacant of all troops to prevent any chance of discovery or suspicion. The tactic was to be a 'Swoop and Capture' plan – that's what Durk called it, but the enlisted me calling it, 'The Swooper'.

Brunswick got his promotion to Master Sergeant because of his prior work in capturing the Christians on the farm. The fact they later got away was not attributed to anything he'd done. If they could capture and even execute the people on this trip he might even look to another stripe – though he knew that was more wishful thinking than likely.

At this time of night, the road was deserted. In fact, such was the case during most of the day. Not many people had cars with gas, and those that did dare not travel in fear of the Goonies. During the entire trip, they passed less than three vehicles, and they were commercial with a guard. What residential traffic there was only occurred during the daylight hours and on main roads. The Goonies seemed to favor the back roads and residential areas where 'hunting' was more fruitful.

At last, their convoy turned down a road near a closed convenience store and gas station. Waiting at the turn was another convoy of trucks with troops. The two officers in charge of each convoy met for a brief conference to confirm all details.

Re-mounting the trucks, they continued down the road until there was a turn to the left. Here, all the troops dismounted and began advancing on foot. The two hundred troops spread out, forming a semi-circle as they advanced on the forest ranger shack and garage entrance to the tunnel. The troops were remarkably quiet – a point strongly emphasized in the training. Once positioned, the signal was given and a group of ten soldiers approached the shack and went inside. They emerged a couple minutes later shaking their heads indicating no one was inside.

Once inside the garage, there was some confusion because they couldn't find an obvious entry to the tunnel. However, that was quickly resolved when one soldier spotted the partially-hidden track for opening the wall and the control box.

Rolling the wall back, they rushed down the drive to the bottom, and then amidst some gunfire, a grenade opened the wall to the inner residences. Some soldiers dashed down the street of residences while another two groups headed down the other tunnels.

Gunfire and another grenade were heard before the scene quieted down. Several soldiers burst into the quarters housing Mary, Tim and the twins. It was empty.

Returning to their officers, they reported that the tunnels were deserted.

"That can't be!" shouted Major Garnett. "Keep going back – they have escaped to the rear – who knows how far they are by now!"

A minute or two later the intercom came to life. "Sir we found an escape tunnel!"

Major Garnett snapped "Get all the men down that tunnel – find where it comes out!" Then, turning to Brunswick the men above to mount up and we'll tell them where to drive in a few minutes.

"Yes, sir!" snapped Brunswick nodding to his aide to take care of it. Although his radio would not reach the troops above, he could contact those nearer the entrance, who in turn, communicated the orders topside. Turning to Brunswick, Garnett snapped, "I'm not going to let these filthy ones get away. Not again. I'll call in as many troops as we need! Stand by here Sergeant, I'm going topside."

With that, he started back at a trot. Brunswick watched him go then turned back and closed his eyes silently hoping they wouldn't try to pin this on him.

* * * * *

Driving the bus without headlights was difficult. What moonlight existed was hidden by the volcanic soot, leaving the bus in deep darkness. Harkins was relieved when he felt pavement come under the bus's wheels. Driving over the soft ground by the creek, he was sure they were going to get stuck, but the bus slowly made its way to the road. On the dark highway, the fastest Sergeant Harkins dared go was forty miles an hour.

The bus was very crowded with all the residents. The seats, which were built for children, were too small to hold the intended number of passengers. But, with some passengers sitting in the aisle and crowded into the rear, everyone fit inside the bus.

"Do you know where we're supposed to go, honey?"

Mary laid her head on Tim's shoulder. "No, not really, just away."

"Hey, Mary," shouted Scott Harkins over his shoulder while keeping his eyes on the road, "Where we headed?"

Mary let out an exasperated sigh and got up moving to the front of the bus. Once there, she stepped down on the entrance steps, so her eye level allowed her to see ahead. "Scott, I don't know yet."

"Well, I'll just keep driving 'til you do," he paused before adding, "Gotta keep an eye on the gas though. We only got half a tank."

Mary nodded. She knew it was important to get off this road for it was only a matter of time until they began looking for them. "The next road you come to turn left," she instructed. Why left? Why not?

Harkins slowed, not wanting to miss the turn in the dark, and it was good he did, for the next road was almost upon them before either he or Mary saw it.

Slowly he turned, reducing to only fifteen miles an hour.

Suddenly, a spotlight went on directly at the bus. The brightness blinded both he and Mary. Harkins slammed on the brakes causing a few gasps from behind.

Slowly, the light moved toward them, then split into two, with one going to the right, while the other to the left. Harkins suspected the only reason they were didn't shoot was because it was an Army bus. He thought about the gun by his knee and wondered if anyone else were thinking the same thing. But, if he acted, how many would survive? The two flashlights traveled slowly down both sides before they heard any commands.

"Everybody out!" came an unknown voice. "Keep your hands on top of your heads and form a line!"

Slowly, they filed off and got their first glimpse of their captors. All were soldiers and one by one the spotlights went out. It took a few seconds for all to adjust to the darkness.

"You all are now prisoners of the US Army," he said loud enough for all to understand. Then pausing asked, "Just who hell are you?"

Chapter 20: The Cleansing

Approaching, the captain looked down at Tim's hand, "Raise your hand!" he snapped. After examining it he looked up, "You don't have a Mark," he said, more in surprise than accusation.

Tim remained silent.

Moving to Mary he had her raise her hand. "You don't either."

Stepping back, he looked over the group. "Who here has the Mark?" he challenged.

His question drew silence which he allowed to linger for several beats. Then turning to his soldiers, he instructed, "You check them all out. Tell me who has the Mark!"

The three men gave their weapons to companions and were about to begin checking when the captain interrupted them.

"Gloves!" he snapped. "Don't you know they may have the Sickness?"

Immediately, three pairs of surgical gloves were produced from a box.

After a brief examination of the group, each of the soldiers shook their heads indicating none had the Mark.

The captain looked at Tim. "How is that possible – are you one of the missing groups of Christians? We were told you had fake marks now."

"We are not part of the missing groups you mean. We just escaped from our camp that was being attacked by some of the troops. For your information, the groups you are talking about aren't missing. We know where they are."

"And where is that?"

Mary did not respond, but smiled.

Suddenly, from the trucks behind, came a hailing voice, "Captain Yetter! It's headquarters! They want to know if we captured any escaped Christians!"

148

"I'm coming!" he shouted over his shoulder then, giving another look down the line of Christians, turned and ran to the radio contact.

One of the young soldiers who had looked for the marks spoke up. "So, you never had a mark?"

"Shut up Hennigan!" came the sharp command from his Sergeant.

Shortly Captain Yetter returned and silently looked up and down the group. "Who speaks for you?" he asked.

Mary stepped forward and quietly said, "I do."

"You do?" asked Yetter with some surprise. "You're the leader? Yetter looked at the line, but there was no reaction. Finally, he said to Mary, "Okay, follow me."

After the captain and Mary left, Tim turned to the sergeant. "The Sickness, what's that?"

The sergeant leaned forward. "You never heard of the Sickness?"

"No."

"It's the epidemic that's sweeping the country. It started in Europe where they say millions have died. You get it, and the next day you're dead – or at least that's what we've heard."

Captain Yetter led Mary to the third truck where there was some privacy. Leaning on the tailgate he asked, "So, you are the head of this group of Christians? You a preacher lady?"

Mary smiled, "No, not a preacher lady. Our preacher is Reverend McDonald, we call him Reverend McDee. He's the short pudgy gentleman on the end."

"That call I just got was from headquarters. They're looking for you – but you know that."

Mary nodded. "Yes."

"By any chance is your first name, Mary?"

Mary smiled, "It is – how do you know?"

Yetter smiled, then chuckled. "Honey, you're famous!"

"What do you mean?"

"Some even call you a Prophet."

149

"Oh, I hope not – I certainly am not that! I'm just trying to help my people out – including myself."

"Well, one of the rumors flying around is that you can remove the Mark."

"I don't do that, only God removes the mark. I'm just the vessel of his blessing."

"So, it's true – you do remove the Mark!"

"Why are you asking me all these questions? Why don't you just take us into prison and be done with it!" snapped Mary, growing tired of the questioning.

If it were time for them to be captured and meet the Lord, then they should get on with it. In fact, within her there was a certain measure of anticipation.

Yetter took a breath then, turning around, took a couple of steps away while considering his response. Finally, he turned and faced Mary. "Well, you see, we are escaping ourselves. We all wanna serve God – I mean we know about God and Jesus and stuff, but we really don't know what to do. Now don't get me wrong, we're all familiar with Jesus and that He is the Son of God, but not much more than that. It's been so long since people have openly talked about God. I mean before these space guys came, I think religion just died a natural death."

"Yes, I know what you mean. I think most people began looking at religion as folklore. Something that weak people use to get them through tough times, or let them keep a positive attitude instead of going nuts in their struggles."

Yetter nodded. "I think the two people who know the most about religion, are a few older folks we have, and they, only because of stories their mothers used tell them. But we really don't know much beyond that."

"And what about you? Are you wanting to become Christian?"

"Yes, I think so. If there were Bibles still around we could have taught each other, but they are long gone."

"So, what are you doing now, where are you going?" asked Mary.

"Right now, we are running. The army doesn't know it yet. In fact, we're supposed to be about fifty miles west of here. We keep the radio going and will until we think they might get wise and send some troops after us."

"So, you know you are under a death sentence, same as us?"

Yetter nodded. He stood there for a second and Mary could see he was trying to make a decision. Finally, he looked at and kneeled. "Prophet Mary, will you make us Christians?"

"Get up!" snapped Mary while looking around. "Don't ever, ever do that again – and don't call me Prophet! Good Lord!"

* * * * *

Durk slammed the desk, and then swept his arm across it, causing everything to fly on the floor. "What do you mean escape? How could they escape?"

He walked to the window and his stride reflected his anger. "Who was in charge of the capture?"

"Major Chris Garnett, sir."

Durk was silent for a moment. "Have him shot – issue the order or whatever you do. I want him dead by sunset."

Sergeant Juska, stunned by the order, remained silent for a moment, finally managing a weak, "Yes, sir." However, he did not move.

"Is there something else Juska?" snapped Durk.

"Ah, well, who do you want to replace him?"

"Replace? I don't care, whoever is next in line," he said, turning around, then whipped back. "Wait. Isn't there a man named Brunswick in this group?"

"Yes, sir, He was just promoted to Sr. Master Sergeant."

"Yes, that's the one. He seems to know something about that group. Make him the commander."

"But sir, he's just an enlisted man."

Durk whipped around. "Are you questioning my orders?"

"No, sir."

"I hereby promote Brunswick to – what was that Garnett's rank?"

"Major, sir."

"I hereby promote Brunswick to Major. Do whatever paperwork you do to make it happen!"

Sergeant Juska hurried out of the office, yet carefully and quietly closed the door. Reaching his desk, he looked at the other sergeants, and half whispered, "Do you know what he just did?" Both Sergeants looked with anticipation.

"He promoted that jerk Brunswick to Major!"

The other two looked at each other, then back at the sergeant. "What?"

"Yeah, now I've gotta send the message out."

The radio message was sent, backed up electronically. The radio operator approached Brunswick with the message. Brunswick grabbed it wanting to decide if it was something he could handle, or pass on to Major Garnett. Carefully, he read the message, and then reread it. He looked up at the radio man, who raised his eyebrows and nodded.

"If this is some kind of joke, I'll have you, and whoever is doing this with you, court-marshaled!"

"Honest, Sarge, when it came through I couldn't believe it. I radioed back for confirmation. They said they are sending confirmation immediately."

"Get me Prefect Durk's office on the line. I need to speak to someone in authority to confirm this. This is nuts! I've never heard of such a thing!"

Brunswick quickly got Durk's office on the telephone. Sergeant Juska confirmed the orders; however, couldn't put Brunswick in contact with Durk because he had left the office.

Very well," said Brunswick after a moment's silence. "Inform Prefect Durk that I am on my way there after carrying out orders here."

Six soldiers were assigned the detail. They marched in silence to the shack being used as field headquarters by Garnett. Entering the temporary headquarters Garnett looked up with an annoyed expression, quickly changing to wonder at the sight of the six armed soldiers and the Lieutenant in command. Brunswick positioned himself behind them.

"Sir," snapped the Lieutenant in charge. "I am informing you that you are now under arrest by order of Prefect Durk and the new commander of this unit, Major Brunswick!"

Garnett rose from his desk, which caused the soldiers to immediately train their weapons upon him, including the lieutenant who drew his forty-five sidearm.

"Are you crazy!" shouted Garnett. "Get out before I have you all shot!"

From behind, Brunswick stepped forward. "It's true. I just got confirmation from headquarters. You are hereby under arrest for failure to perform your duty."

"I demand to be put into contact with Prefect Durk immediately!"

The call was placed, but Durk refused his call. And so, over the profane objections of Garnett, the orders, both of promotion and execution were carried out.

It took Brunswick the best part of three hours to make his way to headquarters. The news of his promotion had been radioed to him and he made sure he confirmed it, but still hadn't recovered from the surprise promotion, or from his first order, which caused the execution of the blindfolded Garnett. But the closer he got to Headquarters, the better he was able to put it into perspective: Garnett's bad luck was Brunswick's good. That's just the way life went. He'd had his share of bad luck and quirky decisions and now he was on the other side.

Good for him. He now had shiny gold Major leaves on his shoulders and the thought made him smile.

He had his driver drop him at the front door to Headquarters. Reaching the office, he opened it and saw the familiar faces in the office. Their looks were not of admiration, Brunswick thought, but of disdain. They had never seen an enlisted man promoted immediately to Major and it wasn't right – not Army.

Brunswick spent many years in their ranks and understood their feelings completely. On the other hand, they would get over it – they had better get over it.

"Is the Prefect in the office?" he asked a bit tersely.

"Yes, sir," was the response.

Brunswick knocked twice on the door and heard a muffled invitation to come inside. Entering the office, he saw Durk sitting at a desk. His two Ancestral Brother aides were standing silently at the opposite corner of the room, as usual.

"Major Brunswick reporting, sir!" he said while snapping attention and saluting, then foolishly dropped his hand remembering Durk didn't like people saluting him.

Durk nodded. "Brunswick, you understand these God people since you were living among them. There's something that's strange about them, don't you agree?"

"Yes, sir. I lived with them for a while."

"How do they keep escaping?"

"If you were to ask them they would tell you it's their God."

"I'm tired of hearing about their God!" shouted Durk getting up from the desk. "Now they are becoming famous! People are starting to hear they are defeating me – ME!" Durk stopped at the easy chair near his desk, resting his hands on the back and regaining his composure. "You have been promoted for one reason and one reason only: I want them dead. Do you understand me – I want them dead!"

"Yes, sir, absolutely."

"So, tell me, what's your plan?"

Brunswick was taken aback by Durk's question. He hadn't really had time to develop one, much less a fool-proof guaranteed tactic to capture and kill the group.

"Well sir, as we speak, I've directed my men to conduct a complete search of the countryside to see if there is any evidence where they might be hiding. I will not tolerate failure."

Durk nodded, "So, you really don't have a plan yet."

"Not completely developed, no, sir."

Durk straightened and turned while staring at Brunswick. "Let me just say this, and make no mistake about it Major Brunswick, you get these people – and I mean in days, or you will be the next one executed. There are a lot of people who would love to have your job."

"Yes. Yes, sir, I know."

Chapter 21: These Last Days

"You say you have become a Christian, and what of your men?" asked Mary.

"Yes, my men believe in God and some know about Jesus. But, when you say, 'all my men', not all are men – I also have their families with me. I have 225 men, women and children."

"Families? You have children too? They are all Christians?"

"No, but they want to be, or at least think they do. Some, including me, know very little about God and Jesus and stuff. There are some who know more than others – personally, as I said, I don't know anything."

"Then how do you know, or your men know you want to be Christians?"

"Well, and this might sound a little crazy, but it began with several of us just having a 'feeling'."

"Feeling?"

Yetter nodded. "Yes, like what we were doing wasn't right. I came to dread the capture of Christians and what we were under orders to do. And then, there were the Christians themselves. They seemed filled with something that gave them a joy even when in jail. Some even sang songs as we executed them. I couldn't believe it."

"You executed some?"

Yetter was silent for a moment before silently nodding. "But some have said that God or Jesus or maybe both will stand for us," he added his voice reflecting more hope than conviction. He paused as emotion grabbed him. Finally, he took a deep breath and continued. "We didn't execute all of them. As I talked with others we began allowing some to escape, then all were free and labeled 'Escaped'. But headquarters started sending messages questioning us, and we knew we had to do something for ourselves and families."

"We talked to more and more of our men and started weeding out the ones who were loyal to those Space Jockeys. It took a while to determine who had or did not have similar feelings. But finally, we did, and when we did, we knew it was time to leave. The boys back at command were becoming suspicious of us."

"So, how did you do it?" Mary asked.

"Well, those who we knew wouldn't go along, in other words, were still loyal to the aliens, we assigned to recon patrols. After they left the rest packed up and headed out."

"You weren't questioned? You were able to just leave?"

"Yes. We talked about it, and we think maybe God just helped us leave."

Mary nodded. "You may be right." Mary was silent a moment. "Do you feel God has forgiven you?"

"We've all talked about it 'til we're exhausted even thinking about it. But we have some who are more familiar with Christianity than others of us. They've told us, because of Jesus, God will forgive us."

"Jesus is able to forgive what we sometimes cannot."

"Are you talking about yourself?" asked Yetter.

"I don't matter; it's you and your men we have to think about now. Where are you going – and what about your families?"

Yetter motioned for Mary to follow him. Leading her a few trucks further back, and pointed inside. Mary saw in the truck and other trucks beyond, women and children huddled together. "These are our families. It took a lot of planning to arrange to have them with us."

Mary smiled, "That's amazing. So now, where are you headed?"

"Just northward, to the national park about fifty miles from here. The park is a several thousand-square-mile reservation. We thought we could camp out in the middle of it, and figure something out from there."

157

Mary smiled, "For the risk you are taking, I would say you haven't got a great plan thought out." She smiled again, "But for Christians during these times, I'd say it's just about right."

"Well, a couple of the men and women suggested that God would guide us. So here we are."

Mary stood silent for several minutes and Yetter did not interrupt. Finally, Mary looked at Yetter. "Tell me, Captain Yetter, what about you – do you believe in Jesus Christ?"

"Yes, I think. I really don't know that much about Him."

Mary was silent for a moment before speaking. "This place you were going, do you have provisions to camp for a couple of weeks?"

"Yes, and if we can find some game, I think we could last a month, maybe more."

"Okay, let's all go there, and we will enroll all of you in Family Everyday Sunday School," smiled Mary.

* * * * *

"Sir," the radio man said, "It's Major Brunswick," as he handed the receiver to Captain Gilbert. "Yes, sir, this is Gilbert."

"Gilbert, I want you and Captain Yetter to widen your circle. I am having Captain Doering come in from the West."

"Yes, sir, however, I haven't been able to contact Major Yetter."

"What are you talking about?"

"Up until yesterday evening we had regular communication, but then it ended. I sent a patrol to his last reported position but was unable to locate him. However, within the last few hours some his men returned to that area from recon missions and were shocked to see he had moved on."

The radio was silent for a few moments except for an occasional crackle before Brunswick continued.

"What's your assessment?" he asked finally.

"Well sir, taking into consideration his past action including some of his transfers," Gilbert paused, "I'm thinking he's gone over."

"To where?"

"To the other side, sir."

"The Christians?" shouted Brunswick.

"Yes, sir, I don't know what else to think."

"Can't he just be lost, or have defective equipment?"

Gilbert looked at the radioman with exasperation before replying. "No sir, I don't think either of those explanations is valid."

"He wasn't one of those Bible-thumpers, I know the man. He thinks the eleventh commandment is drinking!" Again, the radio was silent, and Captain Gilbert had no desire to break it. Finally, Brunswick spoke. "Okay. I don't want to put them on the kill list yet, just put down his unit as 'missing'. Let me know the instant you reestablish contact."

"Yes, sir."

Brunswick hung up and looked at the organizational chart hanging on the wall. Once upon a time, it listed neatly all the commanders and their units – even with pictures, all of which only occasionally changed. Now there were cross-outs with names written in magic markers and no pictures. Even the magic marker names were cross-outs and their replacements the same. All the results of executions or desertions. Brunswick looked at his own name with several cross-outs before it. Would his own just be another of the previous failures? He determined it would not.

Quickly he made the decision not to leave the field command to someone else. If he were to suffer the consequences of failure, he would make sure he was hands-on and not leave the details of an operation to someone else's judgment – or ambition. Leaving his office, he instructed the clerks to keep him informed on an hourly basis of any

159

developments. He then instructed his driver to take him to Captain Gilbert's command.

It was not a small trip, requiring an almost five-hour drive, but as darkness closed in, they arrived at Gilbert's field command. Despite his fatigue from the trip, Brunswick called Gilbert to an immediate meeting.

"Any further word on Captain Yetter?"

"No, sir. I've instructed Able Company to cover the area that was supposed to be Yetter's. It spreads us out a little thin, but least we have coverage."

Brunswick nodded. "You're right, this is desertion. On my drive up here, I instructed all the families of Yetter's troops contacted. Not one, I repeat, not one family was at their quarters."

"So, this was no simple fleeing the field. They planned this for a long time."

"Yes, there are too many moving parts to assume it was on the spur of the moment. So, I'm taking some precautions: All the families of our men are to be moved onto Post and not allowed out. Only troops not on deployment will be allowed to leave."

"All families?"

"Yes, Captain Gilbert, including yours. I've heard other units have done this and it's very effective in cutting down desertions. As we speak all the families of your men are being moved inside the Post. We will build what facilities are necessary to house these extra people; however, I don't expect many new ones will be needed. This command has less than half the personnel it used to have." Brunswick said in a disgusted tone as he walked to a chair and slumped down.

"Captain I'm going to be dead straight with you. My position, in fact, my life – and yours – depends upon our success over the next few weeks. Originally, this command area had over twenty-one million inhabitants, and most of those were Christian of one type or another. The count now is down to a little over ten million. Many of those can be credited to our campaign of weeding bible thumpers out of the population; however, I think we still have one-third who are Christians in hiding. We need to eliminate them as soon as possible."

"Yes, sir, and if I may speak frankly, I think we are spending too much time on this small group of Christians."

Brunswick got up and smacked his hands together. "Don't tell me that! Anybody with half a brain knows that, but you-know-who has some kinda fixation about them."

"I was wondering about an air strike – even a carpet bombing."

"I suggested that already. Planes can't fly with this crap in the air. Plus, and get this, it seems pilots are even worse on desertion than our ground troops. Even if they could get the planes up, they are woefully short on personnel – including mechanics to keep them running. I tell you Gilbert, society is falling apart, and the military is leading the way!"

Brunswick fell silent as he began to pace back and forth in the small room deep in thought. Stopping he turned to Gilbert, "I want you to reduce the men in pursuit of these jerks – but I want some men continuing in the effort. They've got a week to locate and report their position. Who knows, maybe by then I can get them to put a couple aircraft up."

He then went to map of the area. "I want the rest of your men to spread out in squad size groups and start moving back."

He drew his finger across the map indicating the general direction. "You are aware of the new orders from those space guys?"

"Regarding the Christians?"

"Yes, they say some have put the Mark on themselves and are actually hiding in plain sight. Now, here's what I want your men to do. As they are moving back, they are to eliminate every suspected Christian along the way. Do you understand?"

"Yes, sir. How do they do that? I mean if everybody is wearing the Mark, who is true and who is Christian?"

Brunswick paused a moment giving a quick look around as if there might be someone listening. "It doesn't matter. Do understand? It doesn't matter."

"Sorry, sir?"

"Get a clue Captain – not I, not you, not anyone can look into someone's eyes and decide who's Christian and who's not. They're just guessing, right? It's all just a guess."

Captain Gilbert slowly nodded.

"So, stop wasting time trying to determine who is and who is not. We simply tell our troops that everyone in such-and-such area is a Christian or sympathizer."

"Sympathizer?"

"Yes. They may not be a churchgoer, but they know about the Bible and everything. Plus, some who are not Christian but are sympathetic to them and are giving refuge out of humanitarian motives. Look, son, your life, and the lives of your family depend on you doing a good job. I don't plan on having myself shot because I fooled around with conscience. I've been told that the Visitors are impatient. They want to go back to that planet they came from, and I wanna be among those hopping a ride with them. Staying here to die in some natural disaster or on the wrong side of a bullet is simply unacceptable."

Gilbert slowly nodded. "Yes, my wife is really scared about that."

"Well, then help me get this job done. No Mercy."

"Yes, sir, no mercy."

* * * * *

The patrol returned, announcing they had found a place for the group to camp, reporting that it was almost perfect. The location was remote, being seventy-five miles from there. It had a small spring fed creek flowing through it. Though the flow was not much more than an energetic trickle, it would satisfy the needs of the group, if they were patient. Immediately, Captain Yetter ordered them to start moving.

The trucks slowly made their way through the forest knocking down small trees here and there allowing the big trucks to move forward. Finally, they reached the designated campsite. Left behind was a contingent of men whose responsibility to erase any evidence of the trucks passing through the forest. It took more than a week to accomplish this with leaves, branches and some transplants filling in where the wheels made obvious tracks. Finally, the trucks were circled around the creek and Sunday School was ready to start.

Reverend McDee slowly shook his head, "You know Mary, you've got a lot to accomplish. These people know less than imagined. It just amazes me that this could happen. When I was a kid we knew God, Jesus, the Devil – I mean everyone familiar with them. There were Bibles in almost every home. Maybe they weren't read every day, but they were there and respected."

Tim nodded. "Yes, I thought I was God-ignorant, but we have a task here. How did this happen to me, and to them?" Reverend McDee looked around at their group. "If you don't mind, let me take a stab at it. I'm the oldest one here. Officially I'm old enough to be classified as an Old Fart," he smiled. "When I was a child I lived in an average neighborhood, in a typical town in Illinois. Come Sunday, the stores downtown didn't open until afternoon, so everybody could go to church. In fact, there were many stores that didn't open at all, convinced it just wasn't proper."

"Nobody swore in public, it wasn't good form – especially around kids. If we kids heard one of our buddies say a 'bad word', we'd tease him that we were gonna tell his mother," he laughed. "We played all day first one game then another chasing each other around our yards, ending up with a baseball game. The signal we all had to go home was when the street lights came on. At school, we were respectful of our teachers

163

and repeated the Pledge of Allegiance at the start of every school day. Most kids went to church with their parents on Sundays. Those that didn't, and I was one, were supposed to play quietly until the noon hour out of respect – never knew exactly why – for the Lord, we guessed. If a poll were taken of the neighborhood, ninety percent of the people would confess to believing in God in one form or another, and trying to live their lives accordingly. That's the way it was in the forties."

Tim spoke up. "Yeah, I remember my parents telling me about their childhood in the forties."

The others nodded.

"The fifties began the real change, I think," continued Reverend McDee. "Parents began reaping the rewards of their hard work: bigger houses, newer car – but we wanted more, so Moms went to work or continued work – a lot of them had jobs already from the war years. They learned from the big war that women could earn money. It resulted in getting even bigger houses and two cars – they were able to shower their children with good stuff. But more than the material things, we began to drift away from God. We simply didn't need him as much: We had ourselves, and were doing pretty good by us."

"As the years have gone by, we've gained more confidence in our own abilities. We've learned so much more about ourselves, the Earth and the wonders waiting in space. God got a little old-fashioned. We stopped reading the Bible, or going to church, or taking our kids to Sunday School. We simply didn't need God anymore – besides we were working so hard for cars, and houses, and vacations, and clothes, and presents and – well come Sunday, we were pooped."

Roy Kegler spoke up. "Do you think we can teach them in time about God?"

"Oh, I don't think we can do that," interrupted Mary, "But Jesus can. We are only conduits of God's will. He will speak to their souls through our words. Soon, very soon, they too will be free."

From there the conversation drifted to families, and to destination, and speculation about the future. Mary and Tim excused themselves and walked to the stream where they followed the gurgling waters away from the camp. The night was fully on them and the darkness of the forest closed around them. Mary looked up at the stars which seemed multiplied here where their shine didn't have to compete with man's.

"Mary," said Tim. "I'm sure God is pleased with you. Sometimes I feel so left behind as you charge ahead in His work."

"Now, don't go saying that, because we are doing this together. I depend on you to be my strength. I need your arms around me every day. I love God hugs, and I get them, but, just as much, I love my Tim hugs."

Smiling, Tim kissed her on the cheek. "So, tell me, Mary, what lies ahead? Is this it? Is this the end?"

"Not yet; there's a little while to come. I think God has sent out His messengers all over the world to rescue His souls, and we don't have a lot of time to do that."

"So, then what, what comes next?"

"Next… is our End of Days."

165

CPSIA information can be obtained
at www.ICGtesting.com
Printed in the USA
BVHW032154030822
643778BV00013B/364